THEY BROUGHT THEIR WOMEN

EDNA FERBER

THEY BROUGHT
THEIR WOMEN

A BOOK OF SHORT STORIES

Short Story Index Reprint Series

BOOKS FOR LIBRARIES PRESS
FREEPORT, NEW YORK

CONTENTS:

STANDARD BOOK NUMBER:

8369-3339-7

LIBRARY OF CONGRESS CATALOG CARD NUMBER:

70-110188

PRINTED IN THE UNITED STATES OF AMERICA

PREFACE

He is vanishing—that exquisite craftsman who, in white cap and apron, used to ply his trade for all to see and admire through the plate-glass window of the chain restaurant. With what grace he poured the creamy batter, with what dexterity he jerked back the wide-lipped pitcher; what a sense of timing in the flip of the wrist that turned the bubbled surface to reveal the golden-brown underside of the hot pancake. Perhaps tact has all but banished him, or fear or caution. Certainly the hungry man in the street in this Year of Grace must have felt keener resentment, known deeper frustration, as he watched the delicate circlets browning for the delectation of other mouths.

In place of the white cap and sizzling stove there now ornaments the wide window a vase of artificial flowers or a cool and formal edifice of fruit. His passing is, perhaps, just another symbol of a changing world—a world which serves time and digestion with a miscegenetic mixture of tuna-fish sandwich and chocolate malted milk snatched at a drugstore soda fountain.

The American short story of a passing generation was the hot pancake of literature. The same deft pouring of the batter, the same expert jerk, the same neat flip of the wrist at the end.

Nothing in the field of writing dates as quickly as the short story. By its very form and brevity it is restricted from penetrating deeply into the fundamentals of life. The short story attempts, usually, to catch nothing more than a phase, a character, an episode. Profound human emotion demands a larger canvas. It is the material of the novel. To attempt the condensation of novel material into the space of a short story is like trying to stuff a trunkful of clothes into a suitcase. It may, somehow, be jammed in, but it bulges horribly, it refuses to shut quite, it has to be tied with spliced bits of rope, and even then one sees a sleeve, a stocking, ends of cloth sticking out of every corner.

An hour with a volume of one of the old short-story masters is likely to be a depressing experience. The posturings, the windy speeches, the amazing sentiments fall with the effect of utter naïveté on the ear of the reader, bred to the harsher terser style of today. But occasionally a short story is made of stuff so timeless that it survives the test of years and change. For generations De Maupassant's "The Diamond Necklace" has been presented to short-story students as the perfect example of that form of literature. And it is true that in this brief tale the fundamental human emotions are caught with amazing mastery. A woman's seemingly harmless vanity, her utter ruin because of it—a lifetime is compressed into the few hundred words of that story. Hemingway, in "The Undefeated," that touching story of the sick old bull fighter, has managed to give you not only the story of one man's descent into death, but the psychology of a mob's brutality, a nation's

sadism. The bull fight may cease to exist as a Spanish
institution, the toreador become a mythical figure; that
story will be true and poignant a hundred years from now.

Five—six—ten years ago the clever short story, the
story with the snapper at the end, was in vogue. Dis-
ciples of that school sprang up by the thousands. They
seem strangely old-fashioned and unconvincing now.
Yesterday's short story may have, for that matter, a
hollow sound today, if its subject matter has a timely
briskness. Today's fiction writer who writes of his own
time using surface occurrences rather than fundamental
human emotions is likely to find himself in the position
of Alice when she found herself running through the
wood with the Red Queen in *Through the Looking Glass.*

Hot, weary, dishevelled, Alice protested, panting,
that though they had been running and running and
running they seemed to be getting nowhere; that they
were, in fact, just where they started.

"In this country," snapped the Red Queen, "it takes
all the running you can do to stay in the same place."

You need only stand looking out of your window to
see the world changing before your eyes. A revolution,
bloodless or sanguine, is going on in the street below,
whether that street be in China or New York. The king-
dom of today is the republic of tomorrow. This morning's millionaire is a pauper this afternoon. The artisan
is next week's dictator. The writer of fiction finds himself
trying to create in an atmosphere of a three-ring circus,
with clowns, equestrians, acrobats whirling in mid-air.

It is a shifting changing world with an earthquake re-
ported daily, hourly. But the fundamental human emo-

tions, though they may appear harder, less sentimental, are changeless. In Russia today the child belongs to the State, whether born in wedlock or out. If the mother goes to work the child is fed and cared for by State institutions. Now you begin to read that the women of Russia are refusing to bear children for whom they are not permitted to care. Conceiving and bearing are not enough. Women are being arrested for breaking into public nurseries in order to steal their own children. If I were to write a short story of Russia today (which I shall not) I should like it to be the story of a modern Russian girl who loved, conceived, and gave birth in the best manner of the approved Communistic plan—and then stole her child because she wanted to care for it and own it. Russia might change, the Plan fail, the old regime miraculously return. That girl is eternal. Her child is her symbol of perpetuity.

A novelist, temporarily engaged in fashioning a short story, is likely to be apologetic about it. "What are you working on now?" the Pest inquires. "Oh—uh—I'm just doing a short story," the writer replies, as though caught stealing pennies.

It may be, though, that the terrific tempo of the past fifteen years will prove to have been too much for the wind and limb of the novelist. Like the sprinter in the 440-dash who must put every ounce of his vitality into a few brief moments, the short story, crowded into a handful of words, may be the form which has most truly caught the kaleidoscopic picture of our generation.

New York, EDNA FERBER
April, 1933.

CONTENTS

GLAMOUR

EDNA FERBER

GLAMOUR

1932

Edna Ferber

GLAMOUR

O<small>F ALL WORDS</small> in the English (or any other) language, Linda Fayne most hated the word glamorous. Yet invariably the newspapers coupled her name with this shopworn adjective. That glamorous actress, Linda Fayne, they said. Photographs in the magazines showed her glamorous apartment—triplex, with balcony overhanging the East River—and Miss Fayne herself seated therein, attired in glamorous velvet. At her feet was a dog so overbred that all its points seemed out of drawing; lining her walls were books richly dark and oily of binding, picked out with gold tooling that gleamed like the dentistry in a Negro's mouth.

She was, perhaps, the only actress in America for whom a line nightly waited outside the stage door after her performance, just as people used to do in the simple and sentimental '90's, long before her day. All this may have been due, partly at least, to the fact that Miss Fayne, unlike her contemporaries, never dined in popular restaurants, did not avail herself of the pleasant sociability of the red-plush speakeasies, and hated shopping on Fifth, Madison, or any other avenue.

When her Public wanted to see her it had to pay admission or stand out in the cold. It knew her, therefore, through her stage characters, through the newspapers and her publicity department. It was not aware that she liked to dress in old sweaters, easy shoes, and battered bérets; that she worked like a truck horse and practically never had time to sit in that book-lined room overlooking the river, except when she was having photographs done for publicity in her next production.

Sometimes, haggard and spent after a three-matinée week following the merry Yuletide, she would say, as she sipped her midnight cocoa or hot milk, her lean and weary body wrapped in an old flannel dressing gown, "Glamorous, eh!" But she was not bitter about it.

For the past three weeks she had been playing the usual six nights a week and two matinées in *Parrakeet*, which was closing, while rehearsing daily in *Cadogan Square*, due to open in Cleveland the following Wednesday. This pleasing state of affairs was enhanced by four hours' sleep a night and an obsession that she would never be able to play the part.

Linda Fayne lay now asleep, alone, in her bed. It was seven o'clock. The unlovely light of a New York January morning spread its clay-colored pallor over her face. The farther window was open on the river, the curtain not quite drawn. A gray day, and the river flowing sluggishly by was gray, too, and icily thick.

One of the sleeper's long arms was flung outside the coverlet, and the hand was clenched, instead of normally relaxed in sleep. A strange hand to be attached to the lovely body of the glamorous Linda Fayne. Yet not so strange, perhaps; for it was the nervous, lean, big-knuckled hand of the intelligent and masterful woman.

Like most very successful actresses, Miss Fayne was not beautiful. That is, she possessed few of the attributes which the adolescent taste of America usually demands of its beauties. She had a broad, free brow, eyes set well apart and slightly protuberant, high cheek-bones, and a wide scarlet mouth like a venomous flower. The effect of all this was arresting—even startling. So her great following, baffled by this mask which gave the effect of beauty without actually being beautiful, fell back on the trite word, glamorous, and clung to it.

Linda awoke now, not drowsily, deliciously, as one who has been deep sunk in refreshing slumber, but suddenly, with a look very like terror on her face, as though she had yielded unwillingly to sleep and resented the hours spent in its embrace. The instant she awoke her hand reached quickly under her pillow and brought forth a scuffed and dog's-eared booklet, crudely bound in heavy yellow paper and fastened with clips. Typed on the cover were the words "CADOGAN SQUARE."

It contained the seventy-three typewritten sheets of her enormous and overpowering part in the new play now in rehearsal, her own speeches typed in black, her cues typed in red. Any actor will tell you that if you place the script of your new part under your pillow at night the good fairies will help fix it in your memory while you sleep; and that lines conned late at night will stay with you when you awake next morning.

In the gray light of the early January morning she peered at the typewritten pages. She began to mouth words in an undertone. She passed one tense flat palm over her forehead and hair as she crouched over the book, while with the other hand she covered the black-typed lines of her speeches, leaving exposed only the red-inked lines of her cues; and so on, down the page, and over to the next page, absorbed, shadowy in the half-light.

Her cues she mumbled in an undertone, her own speeches she uttered more clearly, but she rocked her body to and fro in the effort of bringing the words forth from her memory, and the whole effect was strangely that of a woman in the agonies of parturition.

"—Then I'd better be off!"
"No, stay here, I can't see him. I don't feel up to it. I can't."

"—told me yesterday——"

"I know. I know. But I really don't feel that I can see him now."

"—showed him into the library, miss."

"But I—I'd much rather not see him."

"—romantic-looking and quite the dandy."

"Is—is my hair tidy?"

She got gingerly out of bed now, shivering a little, closed the window, tied the cord of her pajama trousers a little tighter, and began her morning exercises. Usually she stopped these horrors altogether during rehearsal weeks, but yesterday she had noticed the suspicion of a roll about the waistline.

She marched across the room with a shattering form of locomotion a good deal like the goose step, except that her knees, right, left, right, left, were brought sharply up to her chin as she marched. The typewritten booklet was propped against her pillow, open, and each time, as she passed it, she peered at it and mumbled as she peered and marched as she mumbled.

"—at last! At last!"

"I—I've had to put off the pleasure of seeing you much longer than I wished."

"—looked down on me often before."

"No, really!"

"—top of the wardrobe, and——"

An outsider, chancing upon her thus physically and orally engaged, would have put her down at once as a lunatic. Yet these were stern antics, and the seemingly disjointed sentences were wise, orderly and meaningful.

The dachshund, Blitzen, roused from his pillow, shook his comic length and lurched toward her to join in the game. "Go 'way, Blitz'. Lie down. *Geh weg! Was machts du!*" He stood regarding her with the worried look of his breed.

She thought, fleetingly, of a cold shower, decided against it, and popped back into bed. There, for another fifteen minutes, she mumbled and rocked. Quarter of eight. Ruthlessly she pressed the button that would summon Miss Grassie. Miss Grassie, young, tweed, terribly executive, Bryn Mawr, her secretary, would appear in ten minutes ready to cue her until, exhausted, she rang for breakfast. Chester wouldn't be awake until ten, at the earliest. No four-hour sleep for him.

Wrapping her warm robe about her, she was out of bed again and padding softly up the stairway to the top floor and into a many-windowed room which, incredibly enough, had the effect of being filled with sunshine on this spectral morning. This was, perhaps, due to the fact that the walls and curtains were a warm yellow, as was the hair of the young person seated in a low chair and inexpertly ramming spoonfuls of cereal into her mouth.

"My darling!" exclaimed Miss Fayne, and swooped upon the yellow head. "Mother's precious!" Then, to a stern female domestically engaged at the tiny wardrobe door: "Good-morning, Nana."

"'Ning, madam," replied the stern female, with a look which said, What right have you to come in disturbing our feeding time at this hour of the day? Mother's precious, likewise, showed an absence of enthusiasm about this early morning visit. She peered around the maternal arms to squeal at Blitzen standing bow-legged and friendly and haggard in the doorway. She then made a whirring and puffing sound with her lips, causing a spray of cereal to descend upon her gifted parent.

"Ellen Fayne DAVIS!" chided Nana, pretending to be shocked, but really quite pleased.

Linda Fayne wiped her face with her sleeve and kissed Ellen's cheek just as a laden spoon was halfway to her lips, whereupon Ellen lurched, dropped her spoon, and began to howl.

"Here. Darling. Mother'll feed you."

"If you please, madam, we don't feed her. It's bad for her now that we're training her to feed herself."

"But Nana, look, it's so hard for her. Here's a bit on her ear. She hardly knows where her mouth is."

"Plenty old enough, madam. My last fed herself at twenty months, the MacArthur baby."

"I'm sick of your old MacArthur baby," said Miss

Fayne, in a pet. "Nana, she'll need the heavy white leggings and the fur-lined coat. The wind from the river is like a wet blanket."

"I had intended to, madam."

"Mother's precious. Mother's darling . . . Bring her into my room before you take her to the park."

"Oh. I thought you'd be busy with Miss Grassie, half-past nine, with rehearsal at eleven and all."

"I will. I am. What of it? Bring her in. Whose child is she, anyway—yours or mine!"

Nana's eyebrows, Nana's whole aspect said, Mine, all mine.

Linda Fayne sped back to her bedroom, followed by the careening Blitzen. And there sat Miss Grassie, cap-à-pie, calm, cool, ready for the business of the day. She put out her hand for the typed sheets that Linda had carried with her to the nursery. She pulled the window curtains wide, she drew a chair to the bedside. Miss Fayne sat back amongst her pillows.

"Top of page ten," said Miss Fayne.

"'—you promise me that?'" began Miss Grassie promptly.
"'I promise.'"
"'—very well . . .'"
"'—Shall I go now?'"
"'Please.'"
"'—done to deserve it.'"
"Oh—uh—wait a minute, don't tell me, Grassie—uh—'I had——' oh, yes—uh—'Oh, I had forgotten! You've just

come from the palace. I have never seen the Queen. What is she like?'"

At quarter of nine two breakfast trays appeared in a little procession made up of Walker, the house man, with the light tray, and Millie, the housemaid, with the heavy one, and Blitzen bringing up the rear. Walker in a white coat, Millie in blue linen.

"Mawnin', Miss Linda!" Ebony above the white and the blue, smiling, friendly.

"Dinner at six-thirty sharp, Walker, on a tray up here."

"Anything specially tasty, Miss Linda?"

"No; I——"

"It's going to be a fierce day for you," said Miss Grassie. "Mutton barley broth, very hot, Walker. Lamb chops, creamed celery, chopped fresh pineapple. That's nourishing, but light."

Miss Grassie threw her the next cue, and began to eat the breakfast placed before her on a little table. Miss Fayne caught the cue, fumblingly.

"Oh, God, Grassie, what's the use! I'll never get it. Here it is Friday, we open Wednesday; I don't even know my lines. What'll I do? It's the part. I haven't got it. It eludes me. It——"

"Drink your coffee."

"All right. But go on, go on!"

They went on indefatigably. Miss Fayne ate her

breakfast: orange juice, coffee, a flat dry biscuit libelously attributed to the Swedes and resembling in appearance and taste a confection of baked ashes.

Miss Grassie ate her breakfast: grapefruit, little golden pancakes, hot and hot-buttered; country sausages, toast, coffee. Walker came to collect the trays.

"Mr. Davis awake, Walker?"

"Oh, no, *ma'am!*" said Walker, as though shocked by the question. He handed Miss Fayne a sheaf of letters. Miss Fayne cast a lackluster eye upon them, saw a particularly lurid one marked air mail, special delivery, urgent, postmarked Cincinnati.

"Did you forget to mail that check to my sister, Grassie?"

"Yesterday morning, air mail. It'll be there by now." Miss Fayne tossed the bundle of letters in her direction. "You'll have to start to dress in ten minutes. Fitting at ten, and it will take nearly an hour."

"All right, all right. Go on."

Miss Grassie went on:

" '——married lady for almost a week . . .' "

Twenty minutes to ten. Miss Fayne threw aside the bedclothes, snatched a pair of stockings from a drawer, drew them swiftly up her slim legs. Her head was cocked toward Miss Grassie, her eyes strained and fixed with the intensity of her effort of memorizing. Brown kid pumps, step-in, slim wool dress.

"My dear, my dear, you think I don't understand! Oh, but I do! I do! And I feel for you and pity you with all my heart! I can do nothing to help you. I daren't even advise you. But never lose hope—never lose——"

A quick martial step up the hall, into the room. Her mother, Mrs. Fayne, handsome, dressed in smart dark street clothes, bristling.

"Oh, Mother, I didn't know you were—I didn't hear you come in."

"I came just a minute ago. I went straight up to the nursery. She's already taken her out. I should think when I come in at this hour of the morning I could see my own grandchild."

"But Mother, you know Ellen's always out by nine-thirty."

"What for, I'd like to know! What good will it do her, a bitter, damp, miserable day like this?"

"But she can't be out yet. I told Nana to bring her in to me before she took her out."

"I wouldn't have that woman in my house!"

"She's a wonderful nurse, and she loves Ellen. She knows what's best for her. Ellen's used to being out in the cold."

"Look at you! You're shivering, indoors."

"That's because I'm so terribly nervous."

"Get out and get a little exercise, instead of staying in bed half the morning."

"Exercise! Good God, Mother, I'm on my feet from ten in the morning until two the next morning! Exer——"

A rather heavy man of forty or thereabouts appeared in dressing gown and slippers, a piece of toast in one hand. Handsome eyes, no chin to speak of, a good figure that was losing ground.

"Hello, darling," said Linda Fayne, pulling her hat down over one eye. "Grassie, where's that brown bag? I had it last night. Oh, I know, I left it downstairs on the table in the——"

"What a stinkin' day," said Chester Davis, strolling to the window and looking down upon the river flowing lumpishly by under a gray sky. In passing he had nodded to his mother-in-law, and the two had exchanged looks of richest dislike.

"Everybody living the life of Riley in this establishment," Mrs. Fayne remarked with a false breeziness. "You certainly keep funny hours for a Wall Street man, Chester."

"Wall Street, my pretty, is just a lot of brick-and-stone mausoleums these days. I might as well go and sit in Trinity churchyard."

"Mr. Fayne was out of the house at seven this morning."

"I'll bet he was!" said her son-in-law, very distinctly.

Linda Fayne snatched the paper-bound booklet from Grassie. She thrust an arm into the sleeve of a rather shabby *Breitschwanz* coat.

"Linda, I want to have a little talk with you about your father," commanded Mrs. Fayne. She always spoke of her husband as "your father," when talking to Linda, as though disclaiming responsibility for that erratic gentleman.

"Not now, Mother. Not now."

"When, then?"

"I don't know. Next week. No. After we get back from the road. After we've opened."

"Everyone's more important than your own mother and father."

Walker appeared. "Connelly phoned they's something the matter with the car, Miss Fayne; says he'll be another hour, anyway, fixing it; says——"

"Get me a taxi. Is he on the wire? Tell him the theater at three-thirty; tell him it's got to be fixed by then." She was halfway down the stairs. "Home for dinner, Chester?"

"No!"

"Home at six-thirty?"

"Nope. Playing squash at the club."

Jolts, bumps, skids, traffic jams on the way to the dressmaker's, but she paid little heed except, now and then, for a frantic glance at her watch and another at the maelstrom surging about her cab. Her eyes were on the worn and tattered pages of the booklet in her hand; her lips moved.

Here she was. Ten past ten. Ten minutes late. Connelly could have made it on time. He had secret ways of worming in and out of traffic.

There were three dresses to be fitted, voluminous petticoats, slippers, hats. *Cadogan Square* was a costume play, the period the middle of the nineteenth century. They were ready for her in the big mirrored fitting room. They understood. Madame Renée, head of the workroom, a stout, red-cheeked Arlésienne, sound, hard, astringent as the wine of her own native province; Mrs. Carewe, head of the French room, who wore a hat all day long, and smoked cigarettes at the end of a long holder, and said, "That red is wonderful on you. I knew it would be. Now don't fuss. Everything will be there for the dress rehearsal on Sunday. Have we ever fallen down? Well, then!" And on her knees on the floor little plump 'Tasie, the fitter, a craftsman to whom the figure standing before her was only a structure of velvet and silk and lace and flesh and bone to be made into a perfect whole by the magic of her pins and needle and scissors.

"That is well," said Madame Renée, from time to time; or, "No, no, no! *Le mouvement.* Leave it. You must not break the line!" Like a top sergeant.

Miss Fayne looked up from the pages in her hand. She had been standing almost an hour. "I think it could be an inch longer. It ought to dip the floor all around. It'll be filthy in ten minutes, but it ought to, just the same."

"That's right," said Mrs. Carewe. "And the sleeves tighter at the elbow, but wide at the wrist."

The three women moved around her, around and around.

Suddenly, "Quick!" said Linda. "It's almost eleven. Take it off." She never was late for rehearsal. She was horrified at stars who kept their company waiting. She dashed out, leaving behind her a whirlwind of French adjectives, velvet skirts and muslin petticoats and plumes. No one recognized Linda Fayne, a slim girl in a rather ratty fur coat and a hat jammed down over her hair.

She reached the theater, miraculously, on time; not her own theater, where she was playing at night, but another, untenanted, and available for rehearsals during these past three weeks. She was, in fact, early, for the director, Mr. Ibsen (no relation), had not yet come in. Nesbitt was there, her leading man, that intelligent and responsible young Englishman brought over for the part. There he stood, in a corner, and his head was bent and in his hand, too, was that familiar dog's-eared book of typed paper, and his lips moved, silently. Dear

Nesbitt, with his solemn spectacles on his fair young face, and his pleasant English voice, and his beautiful English trousers and his feeling for the theater and his great good taste in it.

"Good-morning. Good-morning. Good-morning." And then straight over to him. After her performance the night before they had come back to her apartment to go over the third act together from midnight until two, and had parted inarticulate with weariness. Yet here he was fresh, rosy, tubbed-looking. They began where they had left off, without a preliminary word.

"I think I know how we can get around that scene. Let's just try it now, for sight lines, while we're waiting. It came to me after you left last night. Here." They moved to the center of the stage. "Where I say—uh—what's that? Oh, yeah—I say, 'You don't know what he says. You don't know how frightening he can be.' Well, I can turn away from you there, like this. And if you'll sway forward—you won't need to take a step that would break the scene—just sway out and sort of toward me as I lean away, and they'll be able to see you beautifully. Let's try it."

They tried it, solemnly. She turned away, he swayed forward, she put out her right hand, palm out, in a gesture that cut an imaginary line from the lower right stage box to the spot on which they stood. "There! That does it!"

"Splendid!" said young Nesbitt. "I say, Miss Fayne, you're amazing!"

Ibsen came in, brisk, nervous, irritating. He clapped his hands together sharply. "Now, then. Second act. Mr. Logan! Please!" Just as if they had not all been waiting for him.

Miss Fayne and the three other women of the company thereupon quickly tied about their waists flounced skirts of very mussed muslin and crinoline. Part of Linda Fayne's exquisite technique was her insistence on a geometrical study of position. As the play required voluminous crinoline skirts, rehearsals must be conducted with makeshifts of the same, so that positions, distance, sight lines, attitudes standing and sitting might be gauged. The women now moved about, serious, intent on their parts, serenely oblivious of the grotesquerie of flounced crinoline below the stern severity of their workaday sweaters or wool blouses, and their modish little modern felt hats.

An hour of this, broken by stark tragedy in the person of Simon Ludwig, the scenic artist, who entered followed by three men carrying panels of the first-act set. These turned out to be a blue-green which would prove poisonous as a background for Miss Fayne's first-act costume, a purplish red, hand-embroidered, and three weeks in the making.

"But Mr. Ibsen, it's impossible. You must see that.

You see it, don't you, Simon? It would make me look as if I had jaundice."

"But it's the color of the sample we submitted, Miss Fayne, weeks ago, and you approved, and so did Mr. Ibsen and Mr. Wolfe."

"Where's Mr. Wolfe?" demanded Linda Fayne. Oscar Wolfe was the producer.

Mr. Wolfe. Mr. Wolfe. Mr. Wolfe was in his office in Forty-fifth Street, talking long distance to Cleveland.

Miss Fayne became dreadfully calm. "It's foolish to waste toll rates on long distance to Cleveland, because we're not going to open there Wednesday, anyway. We can't."

"Oh, now, Miss Fayne, it'll all be ironed out by the time——"

"When? How? Look at that green! You simply haven't seen my red, or don't remember it. Miss Grassie! Send over, will you, and get a sample of the red to show Mr.——"

"I've seen it. I've seen it. Listen, Miss Fayne. At the very worst you can wear it on the road and order a new one in another color for the New York opening."

Simon Ludwig, looking suicidal, said he might tone down the green, making it more of a yellow-green, but then he certainly couldn't have it ready for the dress rehearsal on Sunday.

The stage doorman. "Say, Miss Fayne, there's a

girl here says she's got color samples of red. She says for shoes."

"Tell her never mind. I'm not going to wear the dress, anyway. . . . Hey, Dolan, wait a minute. I'll just look at them, anyway. Tell her to come here. The shoes might as well be right, even for the road."

Jimmy New, the publicity man, who had been lying in wait to snatch her at the first pause in rehearsal. "Hello, Miss Fayne! Gee, you're looking wonderful this morning. The harder you slave the better you——"

"All right, Jimmy. Let's have it."

"Well, we got to have some new pictures."

"You've got thousands. Millions!"

"Yes, but we want new ones for this play. This is different. I'm getting out an advance story for Cleveland."

"Oh, Cleveland." With the falling inflection.

"And there's a man here from the *Times* wants to make a head-and-shoulders sketch while you're rehearsing. Just a head-and-sh——"

Ibsen's sharp spat of the hands, like a pistol shot for those overstrained nerves. "First act! First act! Everybody! Please!"

The red samples thrust into the errand girl's hand. "This one. Tell Mrs. Carewe this one, please. Thank you. . . . All right, Jimmy. Photographs. I don't know when I can . . . I've a permanent at three-thirty for the new hairdress. He's got to do it. You know. Curls. It'll take almost three hours. Tomorrow. Tomorrow, before rehearsal. No, I've a fitting again at ten. How about tomor—no, tomorrow's matinée. Noon, tomorrow. I won't need any lunch. Head? Oh, the head. Why don't we wait until I get the new hair-do, and then have the *Times* artist do the—— All right, Mr. Ibsen. Sorry."

Another hour of rehearsal. Almost one-thirty. "Only half an hour for lunch, please, ladies and gentlemen. We must get on, and Miss Fayne won't be able to rehearse tomorrow afternoon, matinée day. Everybody back here at two, please." Hober, the stage manager. He caught Miss Fayne on her way out. She and Nesbitt were in the habit of lunching together at the Narragansett Quick Lunch just next door, which was not so grand and not so crowded as Childs, across the way. There, during the half-hour, they could talk over a scene; decide whether today's treatment of it was, after all, an improvement over yesterday's.

"Miss Fayne, that young fella's here."

"What young——?"

"The new boy for the bit in the third act. I think he'll do but you'd better see him. I'll rehearse him, if he's right."

She turned to Nesbitt. "You go on. I'll be there in a minute. Order me a pot of tea—black—and a chicken sandwich, all white. Irma'll understand."

It required five tactful minutes to bring about a state of coherence in the new boy for the bit in the third act, and another five minutes to decide that he would do, with Hober's grinding private coaching. That left a scant twenty minutes for lunch.

Beside the plate of each was the battered booklet, open at Act Two. Irma brought the pot of tea, black. Irma set before her the chicken sandwich, all white. Irma knew that she was serving, daily, at the Narragansett Quick Lunch, the glamorous Linda Fayne, but Irma was too much a woman of the world to take advantage of that fact. Irma, with her yellow marcel wave that seemed cut out of wood, and her disillusioned eyes, and her slim, quick legs. The lights of Broadway were her sun, the Bronx express her chariot. Wise, tolerant, friendly, hard, and urban. To her Linda Fayne was a hard-working actress in a bum hat, and looked like she needed a rest, if you ask *me*. "There's your hot water with it."

"You think of everything, Irma."

"I guess I got a right to know by now." Often Irma's speech was unintelligible to the ear unaccustomed to New Yorkese.

Linda and Nesbitt ate and drank. "How's your little boy?"

"Oh, he's right as rain now. Just a cold. Change in climate, I suppose."

"Did Mrs. Nesbitt find an apartment?"

"Not yet. They do seem fearfully expensive, don't they? We can't manage hotels, you see, with the boy. Not that they're cheap. But furnished flats—really, it's ghastly."

"I'll tell Grassie. With Grassie on the job you'll get something in no time."

"I say, that's kind of you, Miss Fayne."

"Oh, no," vaguely. She was thinking of something else, palpably. "It didn't go a bit better this morning, that scene. And I'll tell you why. It isn't written, that's why."

"It does need rewriting. Won't he do it—Korber?"

"He says it isn't a lack in the writing, it's in the interpretation. Then I ask him what it means and he can't tell me, and then he goes away and sulks and doesn't come to rehearsal, because he can't fix it."

"Perhaps he'll be round this afternoon."

"It's no use. We'll have to try it out on the road, and show him its wrong, and that they won't take it. Then he'll have to do something about it." Two minutes to two. She paid for her lunch; he paid for his. "I'll tell you what I think. I think he has got away from the mood and tempo of his play, in that scene, for the sake of a bright line. It's a good line, and I'll get a laugh on it, but it's out of key. There you are, imploring me to marry you. Would I be likely to wisecrack at a time like that? It isn't in character. She'd say something like . . ."

The musty dimness of the theater enveloped them. Wolfe was there, round, gentle, charming, shrewd. "Oh, Oscar. Where've you been hiding?"

"Me! Hiding!"

"It's no use saying we'll open in Cleveland on Wednesday. The set's wrong, I'm ragged in the part, it needs rewriting; we're trying out a new boy for the first time this afternoon in the part of Charles; my clothes aren't right, I'm rotten in it, anyway."

"All right, Linda. All right. Then we don't open in Cleveland on Wednesday. The thing is, you should be happy. You've got the part of your life here. Last year, you remember, you did nineteen thousand your Cleveland week. You'll do even better this trip. It doesn't matter. We can stay out another week. Cleveland is crazy about you, but you're the one——"

"We'll see. Maybe, by Sunday, it won't seem so hopeless."

Hober at her elbow. "Miss Fayne, the man's here with the couch. He said you wanted to see it today against the green of the set, so that if it wasn't right you'd have time to change."

"Oh, I'm on in a minute. Where is he? . . . Doesn't that seem awfully yellow to you? The sample looked more gold, didn't it? Gold? Of course if Ludwig tones the set into a more yellowish-green—otherwise this would be awful. Still, maybe under the other lights . . . That's my cue . . . 'No! No, Wilson, don't touch me!'"

Three-thirty. The hairdresser. I can't help it. I must go. It's my permanent for the hair-do. Mr. Nesbitt, will you come round after the play tonight? We can get in an hour or so, at my house. Do you mind? That's sweet of you. It's got to come right. Maybe that scene on the couch . . .

"Miss Fayne, will you try this book?" Otto, the property man.

"Book?"

"It's your book in the first act. The real one. I think it's the right weight you wanted it. You better sit down and hold it; see if it feels good."

She sat down. She held it. She leaned back indolently and weighed the book in her hand, and by some miracle it was right, and she beamed on Otto and he took the book and went off, full of other momentous affairs.

Connelly was there with the newly repaired car. He was all for elaborating on the story of his struggles with it. "That's fine, Connelly. You're sure it's going to be all right now? After Tuesday I shan't mind, but just now! . . . Frederic, the hairdresser, on Fifty-seventh Street."

Frederic was waiting with his comb, his scissors, his bowl, his bottles, his bend from the waist, his elbows in air, and his little finger of each hand elegantly crooked.

"I must—I mean, I simply must—be home by six-thirty, Frederic. Now, then, the part. She wears crinoline. It is about 1840, in England. She is not beautiful, but interesting and fragile. Curls, but not a young girl's curls, you understand. A woman."

"Ah! I know. George Eliot!" said the surprising Frederic. "The mind, yet a woman. The story of the play? Just in rough, you understand. It is better that I know, for the artistic result."

She told him. It sounded, she thought, in a panic, rather silly. Silly, too, to be sitting here with her hair being clamped into shining metal tubes, trapped for a period of three hours, and all for a play that might never see a performance.

"Oh, but amazing!" exclaimed Frederic. She had forgotten about him. "You will be ravishing in this play. You will see. Here your hair must be cut more thin on the sides, so. Then here flat, and here more full. You will be like a cameo, exquisite."

"Really, Frederic? Do you really think so?" She felt better. She wondered how she could sit there until after six. Just sit there. But Grassie had promised to come and cue her for these hours of enforced idleness. Where was she?

"Hello!" Grassie's reassuring voice, Grassie's intelligent, cheerful face in the glaring white light of the little booth. "Good God," said Miss Grassie, "if your dear public could see you now!"

"Here." Linda thrust the part at her.

Miss Grassie sat down, pushed her hat on the back of her head. "Last?"

"Yes."

" '—room in the carpetbag.' "

"Oh, say, I think Jimmy's cuckoo. When I told him you were trapped here for three hours he was all for sending that *Herald-Trib* girl over for a special story she wanted to run the Sunday before we open here. And you looking like Medusa."

Panic. "But she isn't——!"

"No. He doesn't even know the name of the hairdresser. Besides, I explained to him why I thought he'd gone balmy. So don't worry. Uh——

" '—room in the carpetbag.' "
" 'Never mind.' "
" '—forgotten nothing else.' "
" 'And if we have, it won't matter much.' "

Five o'clock. Six o'clock. A row of stiff little dark cylindrical curls bobbing like corks about her neck. "But soft, soft!" pleaded Frederic.

"No, I can't. Not till Sunday. I've got tonight's performance to play, and two tomorrow, with my hair absolutely modern. Heaven knows how I'll do it."

The gray morning had kept its promise of a rainy night. The apartment on the river was warm, bright, inviting. New York, Linda thought, aloud, was full of lucky women who would put on garnet-red velvet house gowns to dine cozily at home at seven-thirty, at their leisure.

"Nonsense!" said Grassie briskly. "All tearing into evening clothes to gobble their dinner to get down to the theater to see you at eight-thirty."

"You're a duck," said Miss Fayne.

Ellen had one degree of temperature. It was nothing, madam, Nana said. But don't you think you'd better call Becker? Certainly not, madam. Well, if she isn't perfectly all right by morning. She will be. I'll look in when I get home tonight. We'll be sound asleep.

She took off her clothes and got into bed with a little grunt of weariness and relief. Six-forty. She had one whole delicious hour before she need start for the theater. Snug, warm, comfortable. This morning seemed far away. Years away. She must relax. Her eyes turned toward her bedside table, where her part lay, open at Act Two, Scene One, as she had placed it when she came in. Her hand reached for it.

Walker entered with her tray. She surveyed it listlessly. A bunch of violets on the tray, thrilling as violets are in January. Chester? No. A card scrawled in the great dashing hand that tried to hide a timid, defeated soul. Papa. Henry Fayne. "For My Favorite Actress, from An Admirer." The tears, hot and stinging, came to her eyes. She neglected him. Everyone neglected him. He was that kind of person. He was worth a thousand like her mother, that devil-woman.

"Soup's right hot, Miss Lindy. Don't burn your tongue so you can't say your piece tonight."

The hot thick mutton broth, soothing, revivifying. The lamb chop, creamed celery, chopped fresh pineapple, a little cup of black coffee. She ate it all, gratefully. That was better. There now. A half-hour, almost, in which to rest completely. Try to sleep. That would be wonderful.

No, I can't sleep. It's no use. Turn out the light. There. Relax. Don't think of your lines. Think of being a lake. I'm a lake . . . fluid . . . a lake . . . Open my hands; they're tight. There. . . . My shoulder is tight. Relax . . . There, I'm relaxed. But my mind is tight. I can't make my mind loose. . . .

"Seven-forty-five, Miss Lindy."

On her way to the theater she leaned back in a corner of the car and thought, suddenly, of tonight's performance. It was the first time she had given it a thought during the entire day. It was important. Every performance was important. She was too tired to do it. All that dressing and undressing and going on and being glamorous. If only she didn't have to talk to people. If only they would keep those people away from her. The doorman. She'd have to say good-evening to the doorman. Her maid. That was silly. You're just nervous about the play.

"Evening, John."

"Get in quick, Miss Fayne. They's two girls from New Rochelle High School been waiting since seven o'clock. I told 'em you always come in the front way round so they won't be back here for a while."

"Miss Holstrom here?"

"Waitin'."

Miss Holstrom, the Swedish masseuse, the calm impassive woman with the magic hands. As soon as Linda Fayne was out of her street clothes and wrapped in a dressing gown the electric hands were performing the miracle that would bring the blood away from her head, take the pains of neuritis out of her shoulder. Just ten minutes. Better? Oh, much better, thank you, Holstrom. I couldn't go on without you. Miss Holstrom put on her shabby cloth coat and her mashed hat and vanished with her little bag, like a benevolent fairy.

Cora, her maid, answering a knock at her dressing-room door. "Box office wants to know if they can use your seats tonight, Miss Fayne, if you're not using them for anybody."

"Yes . . . no! No! Tell him no. I forgot. I promised

them to Frederic, the hairdresser. I thought closing tomorrow night we wouldn't——"

Three notes demanding autographs—one from the New Rochelle high-school girls. Suddenly, "Cora, I don't know what's the matter with me. I can't remember my lines. My lines for tonight."

"Why, Miss Fayne, you've played it for ten months and over. You're just nervous, that's all. Now you just relax. I'll open the door; listen for your cue. You just relax. . . . There's your cue, Miss Fayne."

A box of flowers. Dutch pink roses. She loathed Dutch pink roses. A card which read, "Happy memories from Pittsburgh. See you after the show. How about some supper?"

Oh, my God, who were they? Vaguely she remembered that she might have met them, somehow, somewhere, while trying out this play, a year ago, in the West. . . . There they were, after the last curtain. Tell them—in a minute. Yes. Come in. How do you *do!* Yes, indeed. I do.

Two shirt fronts, two silk hats. One red-velvet evening coat, one brocade. Charming. Lovely. Wonderful. Charming. Charming. Oh, I couldn't possibly. I have to work. Mr. Nesbitt. No, not my husband. The leading man in the new play.

They were gone. Get me out of my face. Get me out of my dress. Tell Mr. Nesbitt in just a minute.

She and the young Englishman driving home through the dark cold streets to the river. In the library sounds of voices, laughter. Chester must have brought his friends home with him. She'd have to go in and speak to them.

"Only a second. Do you mind? I'm terribly sorry. We won't even sit down. I'll explain."

In the drawing-room doorway. "Hello! Hello! Come on in, Linda."

"Mr. Nesbitt. Mr. Nesbitt's over here from London to play the lead in *Cadogan*. Have you got everything? Walker will bring you sandwiches in a minute. No, we can't. Really. We've got to rehearse."

Eyebrows lifted. Eyes sliding round.

Up to the little sitting room on the second floor.

"I want to dash up to the nursery just a minute. Ellen had a little cold. No, nothing. You know how they run a temperature the minute they . . ."

Silence, darkness, peace in the room on the top floor. A passing river boat tooted hoarsely in the fog. She tiptoed in, peered at the cocoon in the little bed, felt the cheek, the forehead in the dark. Warm, but not hot. Unnecessarily, she tucked a cover. She tiptoed out, satisfied.

Nesbitt, pacing the sitting room, had an idea. "D'you know, Miss Fayne, I think this couch is a much better shape for our second act than the one they showed us today. Look. Where I lean toward you and run my arm along the back, I think it's just right because it gives the effect, you see, of my virtually having my arm about you without really quite daring to. That other couch has a higher back and the effect is awkward, don't you think?"

They tried it. Solemnly they went through the love scene—pleading, refusal, passion, capitulation, embrace.

"It *is* better!" agreed Linda. "I'll tell you what. I'll simply have this couch sent down to the theater tomorrow, and we'll throw the other one out. This scene's got to be right."

This settled, they ate scrambled eggs and hot cocoa, and Nesbitt mixed himself a highball. One o'clock. Two o'clock. Chester's friends departed, and Chester came upstairs and leaned in the doorway and said, "God's sake, Lin, you look like your own grandmother. You two better call it a day. What have you done to your hair? Those corkscrews! Well, unless the new play is *Uncle Tom's Cabin* and you're playing Topsy, I don't think much of that coiffure, if you ask *me!*"

"Is it really two o'clock? Connelly'll drive you home, Mr. Nesbitt. He's waiting."

After all, it was a favor to her, this rehearsing late at night when she was playing. It was only decent to see that he got home comfortably. She had felt nervous, though, about Connelly, up so late. Still, she herself had been hard at work since seven, and he hadn't. Oh, well. He'd probably be surly tomorrow.

Chester had gone off to his room. "Chester! Chet, did you turn off the lights downstairs?" No answer. She leaned over the railing, looked down. They were burning. Had Millie remembered to take Blitzen out? She went swiftly downstairs, turned out the lights. The library, the drawing room, were a welter of glasses, cigarette stubs, crushed cushions. Well, she simply couldn't cope with that, at this hour.

Upstairs in her own room. A hot bath. That would help her relax. Hot, and lots of pine bath salts. There. Oh, my heavens, I wonder if Grassie remembered to send a telegram to Cissie Reynolds for her opening tonight. Did I tell her?

I'm frightened. I'm frightened. It isn't the play. The play's good enough, except for that one scene Korber's such a mule about. It's me. I'll never do it. Open Wednesday! They're crazy. I won't. I can't. Out of the bath. Her dressing gown. Into Chester's room.

"Chester! Chester!"

"What? What's matter?"

"Darling, I'm so scared."

"Scared of what?"

"You know. Scared. I can't do it."

She was shivering. Her teeth chattered. He drew her down to him. He tucked a corner of the comforter about her shoulder. He was half asleep, and a little tight, and the whisky and cigarettes of the evening party were heavy about him, but he knew the right words to say.

"You're crazy. You'll be swell. Say, you'll knock 'em cold. You always have. You always will."

"Oh, Chet, do you think so?"

"Do I—listen, if you were ever dead sure of yourself in a new part I'd know you were through. You're always like this. Don't you know that? Look at you before you opened in *Parrakeet!*"

"Was I nervous?"

"Jittering! And look what you've done in it! Nobody can touch you. You're the works, I tell you."

"Maybe it's just because I'm tired. Will you come to the dress rehearsal Sunday night?"

"Sure. Sure." He drew a long breath. It was as though sleep could no longer be fought off. He succumbed to it like a child—like Ellen. He was a child.

But he was right. Of course. She would be able to conquer the part, once this week was over. This week, and the next.

She was back in her own bed. Three o'clock. She must get some sleep. She'd be awake at seven, she knew. Rehearsal at ten tomorrow because of the matinée at two-thirty. Rehearsal, matinée, night performance— the last. There'd be flowers, and people and—she must relax. Quiet, now. Open the window. She had forgotten. The river flowed below, mysterious, black.

She crept, shivering, between the sheets and felt with her feet for the hot-water bag. A boat whistled, and she liked the sound. It was accustomed and real and friendly. Somebody else was awake. She reached for the paper-bound typewritten sheets, and tucked them under her pillow, and made a wish, and brushed the little stiff curls of the new hair-do away from her cheek. And slept.

FRÄULEIN

EDNA FERBER

FRÄULEIN

1932

Edna Ferber

FRÄULEIN

Mrs. CARLTON SCHURTZ had everything. In the order of their (to her) importance she had money, position, looks, children, health, and love—of a sort. Two of these treasures she had had before marriage, four she had acquired with marriage, all of them she had possessed and valued for six years. Yet Mrs. Carlton Schurtz did a good deal of tossing and turning on her pillow these days—nights, rather—the while Carlton Schurtz II, in his bed an arm's length away, slept the quiescent sleep of the man of fifty-seven who has had eighteen holes of golf, a massage, a matutinal highball, and two handsome, healthy infants now growing handsomer and healthier by the minute as they slumbered in their airy quarters on the floor above.

Usually she managed to drop off by three o'clock. She awoke at ten, or thereabouts, when Fräulein brought the children in before taking them to the park. Faintly there reached her ears the not-unpleasant sounds of a well-ordered household in a well-built house in New York's East Sixties. Bath water running.

The far-away drone of a vacuum cleaner used discreetly on another floor. The zing of a telephone bell, nipped at the beginning of its third peal. The voices of small children, muted to the tones of a ménage whose mistress must not be disturbed.

Carlton was up at half-past seven, but he was most considerate about it. He dressed in the dressing room. Carlton made a virtue of getting up at half-past seven. Yessir, no matter how late I go to bed, I'm up at seven-thirty. At my office desk by nine. He did not realize that this virtue, if virtue it was, existed only as a habit due to the solid training given him by Mama Schurtz in his boyhood Brooklyn days when he was little William Carl Schurtz.

His name had shrunk as his fortune had grown. William Carl Schurtz, Junior, at high school in Brooklyn. Then, as a very young man, W. Carl Schurtz, Jr. The Carlton had burgeoned with his first million. It was as Carlton Schurtz II, the eligible bachelor of fifty-one, that he had married Nancy Ravenet, of the Charleston, South Carolina, Ravenets.

He had, by this time, learned the American-rich pattern. At certain seasons of the year you went here, you went there. You went to Florida for the Sun. You went to Carolina for the Golf. You went to Virginia for the Riding. You went to Canada for the Fishing. You went to England for the Racing. It was like an army, moving under relentless orders. The ironclad programme admitted of no fairways in the Dominion of Canada; ignored the existence of piscatorial life in Western waters.

Carlton Schurtz had been amazed—had been delighted—to discover how simple it all was, once you had a great deal of money, even though born above the butcher shop in Brooklyn. You made money. Then you listened to what they said. You played certain games at certain times. You talked little, but in dry deliberate tones, with a quizzical look in the eye. You retained enough of your native flavor to win the reputation of being an Original: a judicious mixture of Dawes, Al Smith, Will Rogers, and Artemus Ward.

You sat tight while some terrifically important figure held forth in a roomful of people. Then, drawlingly, in a temporary silence, you boldly disagreed with him. The effect was electric. Finally, you acquired one thing —a horse, a car, a picture, a house, a boat, a mistress— that was, of its kind, more precious, more nearly flawless, than any other of its kind in the world.

"Carlton Schurtz—you know, he owns the Oompah." Or Streak-o'-Lightning. Or Sea King. Or grows black orchids.

At fifty-one, then, Carlton Schurtz had become so secure that he was unsafe in such open hunting grounds as Asheville, White Sulphur, or Palm Beach, infested

as these spots were with carnivorous mothers of mar-
riageable daughters.

"Come in any time, dear Carlton," the mothers said,
a glitter in the eye. "Don't bother to phone. You're like
one of the family. There's always a bed and a plate."

"You are too kind," Carlton replied. And he meant it.

Daughters said, "I'm so sick of kids with hip flasks.
It's wonderful to talk to somebody like you, who under-
stands. You're like an older brother or a——" Panic.
Blushes.

"Father?"

"Oh, no! I wasn't going to say father at all. I almost
said——"

He never finished the sentence for them. He knew
that for less than that men have found themselves se-
lecting cuff links for groomsmen at Cartier's.

It was when he was golfing discreetly in the protection
of the magic ring made by the magnificent live oaks
encircling Yeaman's Hall, just outside Charleston,
that he met Nancy Ravenet, slim, ashen-blonde,
anæmic, twenty-six. Nancy was so Charleston, so
French Huguenot, that she did not even bother to talk
with a Southern accent. She left that to eighteenth-
century upstarts from Virginia, Tennessee, and North
Carolina.

The Ravenets had a great deal of fine old family,
handsome old mahogany, beautiful old silver (very

thin) and linen sheets and damask tablecloths the size
of a carnival tent, exquisitely darned in patches as big
as your palm. These, together with Miss Nancy, were
contained in the lovely crumbling Ravenet mansion on
the Battery.

Miss Nancy herself was good and sick of all this
ghostly splendor. She was tired of homemade underwear and impecunious Charleston beaux, all of whom
gave the effect, somehow, of wearing black satin stocks
and looking like Lafayette in modern (but not very
modern) clothes. Layer by layer, like the choicest
sweets in a box of candy, these had offered themselves
for Miss Nancy's taking. Layer by layer she had re-
jected them, and they had been gobbled up elsewhere.
She hoped for richer fare, but the years slipped by and
now she was twenty-six, and the box held only those
moldy uninviting items vulgarly known as spit-backs—
green bonbons with a tooth-mark on them; candied
violets; hard pellets covered with tarnished silver
coating.

The adjectives "beautiful" and "Southern" have
learned automatically to leap into position behind belle.
But Nancy Ravenet was beautiful, and she was Southern, and she was a belle. She was not one of your black-
haired, smoldering jujubes. She was all creamy, like a
magnolia. Her pale gold hair was like thick smooth
yellow cream, and hers was the cream-white Southern

skin about which so many poets have so romantically sung—and which is due to the habits of eating hot breads, sitting in dim, jalousied rooms, and taking no exercise. Her languorous manner was largely anæmia.

When she met Carlton Schurtz II she did not raise her Southern voice in accents of vivacity; she did not lift a finger; she scarcely fluttered an eyelash. He dined at the Ravenets' and was served beaten biscuit, which he found completely indigestible, and tough old chicken and homemade wine, and said he hadn't eaten anything like it in years—which certainly was true.

He got, by some magic wangling, an invitation to the St. Cecilia Ball and saw her there queening it in an evening dress so shabby that, even in that collection of dated finery, it stood out with a kind of splendid distinction. Carlton, the rankest of outsiders at this almost sacred function, had difficulty in getting a dance with her. She drifted dreamily off, in dance after dance, with this or that lafayette. Carlton Schurtz, in his London clothes, stood in the ballroom doorway, his eyes suddenly misting (sentimental Negro music and bad punch) as they followed the shabby figure of distinction moving languorously about the dance floor.

"An emerald," he resolved, his gaze resting a moment on her ringless left hand against a black coat sleeve. "Square-cut, the size of a Bronx-express headlight. Black velvet by Worth. Gray crêpe, with handmade collar and cuff things, by Molyneux. Dull green tea gowns. Schiaparelli sports things to watch me drive off from the first tee. One whole closet for shoes and another for hats. Stockings you can stuff into a thimble."

For he, with his millions, had been around by the time he was fifty-one.

Twenty-five years older than she, but not too unattractive. Bald, eyeglassed, but a fair waistline saved by golf, massage, and the New York Athletic Club. The sun—when sun was available—and the sun-ray lamp when it was not, gave him a look of tanned health the year round.

His nails were too well manicured. He was terribly neat. He wore a dark burgundy dinner suit at home. A house in East Sixty-seventh Street. A house at Southampton.

If Camilla, now aged three, had been a boy, there would have been no Camilla. Carlton Schurtz, in his mid-fifties, must have male issue to prove his virility and satisfy the egotism of an old bachelor who has married a young wife. Like a last amazing floral set-piece of fireworks terminating an evening of conventional skyrockets and Roman candles, Carlton Schurtz III was produced to the accompaniment of rapturous oh's and ah's. Then darkness. The entertainment was ended. Camilla, three. Carlton III, eighteen months.

As Mrs. Carlton Schurtz opened her eyes on this particular March morning it was to the dim consciousness of something not quite pleasant lying in store for her today. She lay a moment, still half asleep. The room was pleasant, orderly, accustomed. The angular rods, tubes, slabs, and metals of the modernistic had no part in this room of soft curves, of blurred chintz, of cushions and curtains and gleaming taffetas. The French windows opened on the garden at the back of the house.

The day, she saw, was one of those fantastically blue-and-gold April days with which New York, the show-off, occasionally struts its stuff in March. When Mrs. Schurtz pressed the enameled knob at the side of her bed, her breakfast tray would appear. All this she saw and knew. Still, the heavy-hearted half-consciousness.

Today—something—something not quite pleasant. Today—oh, yes. It came over her, depressingly. Today was Fräulein's day out.

During the week Mrs. Schurtz was hardly conscious of Fräulein Berta's presence in the household, except as an admirable machine that functioned perfectly. It was on Fräulein Berta's day out that her presence made itself felt. On Fräulein's day out, Mrs. Carlton Schurtz, inexpertly assisted by Millie, the parlor maid, was in charge of her offspring from two in the afternoon, when Berta left, until midnight, or thereabouts, when she returned. It required all the following day to re-store Mrs. Schurtz to a normal state of nerves, health, and self-respect.

"I don't know how she does it," Nancy confessed to her husband, at the end of these nurseless days. "I follow her routine exactly. I do every single thing that she does—food, nap, park, bath—everything. And they behave like fiends. Perhaps it's because I love them too much. Children sense these things in electric waves."

"Maybe she drugs 'em," Carlton suggested.

Whatever the cause, certainly the Schurtz cherubs became demons the moment they opened their eyes after their afternoon nap to find their lovely parent bending over them. They were like spirited horses who sense the inexpert seat in the saddle. Fräulein was able, day after day, to stuff incredible masses of food into them—lamb chops, mashed vegetables, stewed fruits, eggs, cereal, milk, junket, bacon. Under their mother's loving eye Camilla messed her food round and round on her plate, and even dropped plops of it on the nursery floor, while Carlton III flatly refused to perform the act of swallowing but allowed his cereal or his egg to drool out of the corners of his mouth and down his chin, a revolting sight. That rosebud orifice, opening like an obedient flower at Berta's behest, now became a maddening, twisting trap.

True to the daily ritual, Mrs. Schurtz, with Millie,

took the children to the park in the afternoon, choosing a spot near—but not too near—the nursemaids with whom Fräulein consorted on her workdays. Long before the allotted time you saw them returning to Sixty-seventh Street, tired, disheveled. The children had a wild gleam in their eyes. Sometimes (when they had been particularly devilish) Nancy Schurtz thought it was a glare of actual triumph.

Bath time was as bad. Camilla threw her new white shoes into the tub. Carlton III slapped his mother's magnolia cheek with a wet, soapy, and astonishingly forceful fist. They howled.

The Schurtzes never went out on the evening of Fräulein's day off. Nancy wore one of her softly gleaming house gowns and dined alone with Carlton, looking pale and drooping and flower-like, as always—a magnolia gone a little brown around the edges.

Mrs. Schurtz did not mind staying home on the evening of Fräulein's day out. She would have liked it better, perhaps, if she could have spent the evening alone. She had very few evenings alone. She and Carlton went to the theater. They had friends to dinner. They dined out. They played bridge.

Carlton had made hundreds—sometimes she thought thousands—of friends in those fifty-one years of his bachelorhood. He was loyal to all of them. He took for granted that Nancy would like them all. Sometimes she thought longingly of the crumbling old house on the Battery, and the shabby lafayettes, and the wild-turkey dinners of her Charleston days. The house had been sold to Northerners.

She was, though she never confessed it to herself, bored. She was bored with the everlasting dinners, and the Schurtz friends, and the emerald as big as a Bronx-express headlight, and the velvet house gowns, and having her hair waved and her nails done a deep rose. She was bored, in a word, with Carlton Schurtz II, though fond of him. She was luckier, she knew, than most women. She urged him to go down to Asheville or to White Sulphur for the golf. Alone.

"It will do you good. You look sort of washed-out."

"I need a shave."

"Nonsense. You've been looking fagged for a month."

"When do you want to go?"

"Oh, I don't want to go. You. Besides, I wouldn't leave the children. All this flu around."

"Fräulein'll handle them. She's a wonder, that girl." Carlton stood a moment, collar and tie in hand, as though struck by a sudden thought. "What a life for a young girl! She can't be more than twenty-three. Taking care of somebody else's kids, stuffing food into 'em and wiping their noses. A good-looking girl, too. Fresh-looking." Unconsciously his gaze rested a moment on Nancy, seated before her dressing table.

Nancy selected a bracelet from her box, slipped it on her wrist, surveyed the effect, her hand and arm outstretched in the immemorial gesture that Helen used, and Cleopatra, and all women who have been decked with jewels by men.

"She isn't bad-looking, really, in a wholesome, peasant kind of way. Of course her cheekbones—and those thick ankles. I think, given a choice, that I'd almost rather have an ugly face than thick ankles."

"Are they thick? She just wears those sensible shoes, doesn't she? Working?"

Nancy glanced down at her own slim, delicate feet. Her ankles could be encircled with a thumb and second finger.

"They're sensible, goodness knows. So is she. And a little thick, too, like her ankles. I suppose if she weren't she couldn't stand it, poor thing. I wonder if she ever has any fun. I don't think she even has a beau. What do you suppose she does, from two until midnight, on her day out? Goes and sits with some friend, I suppose, who's taking care of somebody else's children."

Carlton laughed appreciatively. "Busman's holiday."

Some of these thoughts were drifting through Nancy's mind now as she finished her breakfast. There was a scuffling sound at the door, voices, then a firm little rap.

"Come in!"

Fräulein, with the children. Suddenly the quiet dim

bedroom burst into a thousand sparks of light, color, sound. Camilla, in broadcloth and fur and leggings, looking perversely like Carlton II; Carlton III, in broadcloth and fur and leggings, looking like an exquisite edition of Nancy. Their faces glowed, bloomed, seemed to give out actual light. The whites of their eyes were a healthy blue.

Fräulein brought them to the slim pale figure in the bed. There was about Fräulein a quiet vitality. She did not bustle. This vital quality went from her body in warm, sustaining waves. The children felt it, thrived on it. You rested on it, drew life from it as from the earth when you throw yourself upon it, gratefully, in the first days of spring. Both blonde, Nancy's blondeness, beside Fräulein's, was that of an exotic orchid beside a sturdy plume of stock.

"Oh. Hello, darlings. . . . Don't *do* that, Camilla dearest. Mother has a tiny headache this morning. . . . Did you put the drops up his nose, Fräulein? . . . You don't think he ought to stay in the house today with Millie, do you, while I take Camilla out? . . . Well, I just thought . . . Oh, is it? Just the same, it isn't spring yet—not really, I mean. This is the dangerous time of year, when it's too warm for winter things and too cold for summer—and I'd hate to have Camilla catch Carlton's cold. . . . Well, whatever it is. . . . I—uh —suppose you wouldn't want to stay in today just until four, instead of leaving at two? I just thought if you hadn't planned to do anything special."

"I have planned," said Fräulein. She spoke with the least trace of an accent. Her *v* was likely to be more *f* than *v*. Her voice vibrated now with a strange intensity.

"Oh. Well." Privately she thought—planned, fiddlesticks! Planned what!

Carlton on her arm, Camilla by the hand, Fräulein moved toward the door. The room seemed close. She longed to be out in the crisp air. She was dressed for the street, as were the children. She descended with them in the little electric lift. Carlton puffed out his cheeks and made big eyes and pounded the brilliantly painted metal walls with his soft fist. He was feeling the spring. Camilla leaned against Fräulein's thigh for balance. She did not like riding in the lift.

"So!" said Fräulein, stepping out at the street floor. "The park, the park! In the sun, the sun!"

"Park the park in the sun the sun!" echoed Camilla, skipping. Carlton III, catching the spirit of the thing, squealed.

Frederick was dusting the hall. For the past twenty minutes he had been dusting the hall, which contained three articles of furniture. Fräulein was fifteen minutes past her usual schedule. The drops in Carlton's nose.

He stood in their way. His eyes glowed. He put a hand on Camilla's head, patting it. The hand would have trembled had it not patted. "Are you off today?"

"What do you care?"

"I'm off, too, after dinner tonight. They're only having two, for bridge, after dinner. Millie will serve them. We'll go to a movie. Will you? A dollar one, downtown."

Fräulein shook her head from side to side.

"Why not? Why not? You haven't got a date." This was bravado.

Fräulein shook her head, up and down, this time.

"With who?" He transferred the hand from Camilla's head to Fräulein's arm. The fingers tightened. "With who? Not with that wop! That greasy mechanic —that Louie!"

"Co-*mon!*" whined Camilla, tired of the dark hallway. She jerked Fräulein's skirts. "Co-*mon*, Fräu'n."

"Yes, my darling." She plumped Carlton into his English pram, tucked the rich robes about him.

"Berta! Answer me."

"I have an engagement."

"Yes. All right. But is it with him? Is it——"

She opened the front door. There at the curb stood Louie, the chauffeur. He was doing something to the car, with his eyes on the front door. When he saw Fräulein he pinned down the engine hood and sprang to help her as she bumped the heavy pram down the two steps to the sidewalk. A tall, thin Italian with a scar on the left cheek. His uniform—tightly fitted and buttoned coat and smart cap—gave him a false air of distinction.

"I'll drive you over to the park," he said. "The madam don't want me till eleven."

"The baby's buggy."

"I'll put it in the front."

"I'd rather walk. It's only three blocks. It's healthier. Such a beautiful morning."

She turned toward the park. Louie followed her. Frederick, in his work apron, stood helpless in the doorway gazing after them. Camilla trotted by Fräulein's side. Fräulein's hands rested lightly on the pram handle.

Louie glanced sharply round at the discreetly curtained house windows. Then he put one lean brown hand over one of hers. "Listen, golden-haired darling. They are at home tonight. I am off. We'll go to dinner —Italian, with red wine, at Salvatore's. And a movie."

She shook her head.

"A show, then. A real show, with dancing. Or we could go somewhere and dance. Roseland."

"I can't. I have a date."

The dark face grew darker. The scar leaped out, queerly purple. "With that Austrian? With that Frederick?"

"It is no business of yours who with. You must go back. If the madam sees you like this from the window!"

They had reached the corner. She grasped Camilla's hand, looked right and left, smiled at the corner police-man, received his nod and wave to come on, made a dash for it. Louie stood a moment on the curb; turned, defeated, his smart black boots glittering in the sunlight.

The East Sixties and the East Seventies were dotted with nursemaids stepping briskly along toward the park with their charges. They wore good cloth coats with real fur collars, thick and soft; and smart felt hats and good gloves and silk stockings and excellent shoes, sometimes with trim galoshes over them as protection against the nipping cold. They were the most expen-sively dressed nursemaids in the world. Everything they wore was good and modish. They and their charges had been up since seven. They were all full of prunes and cereal and bacon and toast and milk and orange juice.

An April day, gone completely mad, had leaped ahead of its fellows and plumped itself wantonly into the lap of March. New York was sharp-cut in outline. The high white buildings pierced the blue of the sky. The Pierre, at Sixty-third, dazzled the eye. The trees in the park had not yet budded, yet to the knowing gaze there was discernible just the faintest hint of swelling along the branches etched against the blue.

Fräulein's sentimental Teutonic soul could stand it no longer, what with the signs of spring, the importunings of butler and chauffeur, and the prospect of the day ahead of her. She must find relief in poetry.

> "'. . . das Saatkorn dort, und wartet still,
> Ob's wieder Frühling werden will.'"

She looked up at the trees. She looked down at Camilla. She gave a little skip and a rush with the pram. "*Frühling! Frühling, mein Kind*," she trilled.

Camilla skipped, too, catching the spirit of the thing. "Fweeling! Fweeling!"

Life was very agreeable, Fräulein thought.

She had her special little place in the park, where her exclusive coterie of nursemaid friends forgathered. They were very snobbish and select. Their charges were all children of the rich. These played primly on the cement paths, or slept in their perambulators. They wore tiny fur coats, miniature editions of the pelts in which their mothers were swathed; and white or pale blue broadcloth leggings and chic bonnets to match. As you strolled past the little group in the lemon-yellow spring sunshine there came up to sensitive nostrils the scent which—next to new-mown hay—is in the whole world the most pure and exquisite: the scent given out by the flesh of very small clean babies.

They were all there, for she was a little late—Fräulein Lotta and Fräulein Hedwig and Fräulein Carola and

Fräulein Greta, and Mademoiselle Marcelle, and Miss
Peake in her English uniform of blue, with cape and
veil, *fesch* but silly, that uniform, Berta always thought.
Quite an international little group. They looked very
blooming, these girls, for they were out of doors every
day from ten to twelve, and from three to five, sitting
or walking in the brilliant New York sunshine. In the
winter their knees, as they ranged along the park
benches, were snugly tucked in warm woolen robes.

They conversed in English, in German, in French—
but mostly in English. They talked of their employers,
they talked of their households, of international politics,
of economics, of books, of the *Valuta*, of this mad
America, of their memories of Europe, of their parents
in the old country. All this interspersed with calls or
commands to their little charges trotting about the
confines of the park path.

"I have got off today."

"I wish I had. Such a day. What will you make?"

"Oh, plenty."

"He's got off, too?"

"Sure. Every two weeks, only."

". . . fighting in Düsseldorf on the streets. It was
never like that in the old days of the Kaiser."

"Kaiser! That old *Narr!* He made all the trouble."

"They are like children here in America. They play
golf and backgammon and ride around in automobiles

going nowhere and drink out of bottles gin and whisky like coachmen, when the whole world is falling in pieces. Well, they will fall, too."

"*Was machts du denn! 'Wirst schmutzig! Komm 'mal hier, du!*"

"Ca-mee-la! Give it to him back! But yes, I say! It belongs to him; give it to him back. Play with your own dolly."

"She gets a new fur coat for summer, my madam. Did you ever hear of such foolishness!"

"Mine works on committees now and says it is sinful to buy new clothes. I thought she would give me that dress with the white satin tie, but no, she wears it."

They sewed. They read a little. They scrutinized the world going by, and commented on it—plump matrons bound for the two-mile walk around the reservoir; a boy and a girl deep in their own affairs, the boy talking, talking, his voice low and urgent, the girl listening with bent head; rheumy old men, shuffling by in the sun. Sometimes their men friends, temporarily free, or unemployed, strolled round to chat with them. But this they discouraged. They did not approve. It was common.

Twelve o'clock. Like so many noonday Cinderellas, they rose and vanished.

Fräulein kept a sharp eye out for Frederick and Louie. She did not want to encounter them again. The silly fools.

Dinner in the nursery—meat and vegetables and junket. The children ate well, and obediently, not playing with their food as they sometimes did. *Gott sei Dank*, she would be out by two, or even one-thirty, if they fell asleep quickly. Would she wait until four! Ha! That was good, that was. She, too, ate her good, hot, nourishing dinner from a laden tray in the nursery.

Now they were in bed, each tucked in a little downy cell, Camilla in a pink silk cell, Carlton III in a blue. She tried not to communicate to them the waves of her own inner excitement. That would keep them from sleeping.

There. They slept. Full of food, they slept, their arms above their heads. Berta, too, was fed, not only by good food but by the warmth of their sturdy growing bodies, by the velvet touch of their clinging fingers, by their trust in her, their nearness to her, their very demands on her. She gave to them, but they, too, gave to her, and sustained her. The sound of their soft rhythmic breathing was like music in her ears.

Fräulein dressed quickly. Her best coat, with the real fox fur collar, that She had given her, and the smart tight hat that exposed one whole side of her rich golden hair, and her Christmas gloves and her strap slippers with the high heels that made her ankles look quite slim. She had seen people on the streets—on Park Avenue and Fifth, with straw hats already, in March and even February. Let them, the simpletons. She had better use than that for her money.

There. She was dressed. It was not yet two. The door opened and She came in. "Oh. Fräulein. Are you going al——"

"Sh-sh! Please. They are asleep."

"But——"

Fräulein's blue eyes blazed. She tiptoed swiftly toward the door, ushering Her through it by the very force of her resentment, closed it firmly, soundlessly, behind her. "Everything is done. They are sleeping. Their milk is in the ice box ready for them at three. Take it out fifteen minutes before, so it is not too cold. The drops in Carlchen's nose before he goes to bed . . . Scraped apple . . . no egg . . ."

She was gone. As nurse, she was entitled to leave through the front door, but Louie knew this and Frederick. She would go through the service door and fly up the street toward Madison, giving them the slip. They would be watching the front door. She stole toward the kitchen. She was early. Perhaps they still were there. Voices, high, in argument or anger. She stopped, listened.

"Yeah, wouldn't you like to know!" sneeringly. Frederick's voice.

"Go on, Dutchy! She's meeting me at seven, and what do you know about that!"

"Lying wop!"

The clatter of a knife or fork thrown down violently among the china; the sound of a chair pushed back, scraping, against the floor. Slap! A little yelping scream. Cook's voice. They were fighting! Frederick and Louie were fighting over her! She turned, fled, up to the front hall, out to the street, up toward Madison Avenue. Her eyes sparkled. Her lips were parted in a smile. Two men fighting over her. Poor sticks they were, and that Louie had a wife, and both were beneath her notice, but men, nevertheless, young and personable. It gave one a feeling of power.

She took the Madison Avenue street car. She was not used to walking in these high heels, and then, too, she must save time. She got off at her bank corner, and went in and sent the usual monthly money order to her mother in Germany. Ten good American dollars. Here in America ten dollars was considered nothing. There it would buy the old people meat, and heat and clothes, even. It meant the difference between comfort and starvation. She knew.

Over to Fifty-ninth Street. In the big block-square department store she did a little wise, scanty shopping. A pair of silk stockings, fifty-nine cents, very good. A suit of men's pajamas, blue, and a man's necktie at the sale counter. Men should wear blue. It made their skin look clear and fresh. She paid for these, took the bundles with her. Over to the Five and Ten. A comb, a spool of white thread, a little packet of tacks, and a yard of oilcloth shelving in a bluebird pattern. The aisles were packed with women pawing over bead necklaces, ribbons, candy, bracelets. She eyed them contemptuously. Throwing away good money.

She took the subway to Ninety-sixth Street, walked back a block to Ninety-fifth and entered a huge brick modern tenement that was a hive for human beings. Her strong young legs made nothing of the five flights up which she must walk. Down to the very end of the long, prisonlike corridor with its double row of shut doors.

She took the key from her purse, unlocked the door at the end of the passage, closed it, locked it again. She stood a moment, looking about her. Her back to the door, she shut her eyes a moment, as if in ecstasy, breathed deeply, opened them quickly as though in fear that the sight before her might vanish.

A small, square, low-ceilinged room, clean, bright, but untidy. Two good windows facing south. The March mid-afternoon sun came in beneath the partly drawn shades. The shades were a little awry, one up, one down. Her bundles still in her arms, she marched toward the windows, threw them open, straightened the shades.

A double bed, unmade. A table, with books and

papers and a green-shaded lamp, A shelf with books. A commode with drawers. A comfortable armchair covered neatly with cretonne. Fräulein had covered it. Two straight-backed chairs. The floor was bare except for three small rugs made of carpet-squares that had been scoured in soap and water, very bright.

Fräulein took another long, deep, soul-filling breath, tossed her packages on the table and plunged in. She took off her dress, her corset, her high-heeled shoes, her stockings. From the closet she took an enveloping work apron and a pair of loose old slippers. Then, barelegged and unstayed, she snatched the covering from the bed, rolled the sheets into a ball and tossed them to one side, turned the heavy mattress with a single gesture of her strong young arms. She placed the stripped feather pillows on the sills of the open windows, to catch the sun.

Leaving the bed to air, she sprinkled some clothes which had been left rolled up in a dry wrinkled ball, for ironing. She washed out two sets of pajamas and some handkerchiefs and underwear extracted from the laundry bag on the closet door, turned the laundry bag inside out, hung it at the window. She went into the tiny bathroom, cleaned and dried the safety razor that lay there, gathered up various small scraps of soap and threw them into a scrub pail.

Next she washed some dishes found, unwashed, in

the corner of the room, back of the screen. She attached a small electric iron, ironed the clothes, pressed two pairs of trousers, made up the bed with fresh linen, wiped up with luke-warm water and soap every inch of floor—main room, bathroom, closet. She wasted no step, no gesture. She was like a terribly efficient machine.

In a corner, on a stout little table behind the screen, was a five-gallon crock. This she inspected minutely, sniffing its brownish aromatic contents. It was still fermenting a little. By day after tomorrow the beer would be ready for bottling. She must tell him. Otherwise it would lose its good strength.

That reminded her. She went to the tiny tin ice box. A little cube of ice, and on it two bottles of beer, a little butter, a packet of thin ham slices. He remembered everything.

Half-past four. Otto would be there at quarter after five. She peeled off the work apron, bent over the basin in her underthings and washed her hair. She dried it feverishly, tossing it, rubbing her scalp with a dry towel. She twisted it, still damp, into a knot (Otto would not let her bob it), and bending over the absurdly small bathtub that was little more than an enameled box, she scoured it with powdered cleanser—tub, faucets, waste plate, pipes, everything.

Otto was neater than most men, and very clean, but

all men were alike. Still, she thought of old Schurtz, and her nose wrinkled. He was neat, too, old Schurtz. He perfumed his handkerchiefs and was quite the dandy for Her. He wore beautiful silk pajamas that were made for him, measured, like a woman's dress, and fresh bed linen on his bed every night.

"I would rather have Otto in a *Nachthemd* made of flour sacking," she thought, "than that old one with his silk and his sweet-smelling stuff. I wouldn't be in Her shoes, not for any money."

She bathed. She lay in the warm water, relaxing. Out she jumped, rubbed herself briskly with a rough towel, put on a bright wrapper she had taken from its hook in the closet, slipped her feet into coquettish mules, let down her hair to dry, took a last comprehensive look around. Bright. Shining. Orderly.

She was deliciously relaxed and a little weary, but the weariness was delicious, too. She lay down a minute on the bed; flung herself across it, the mules dangling. The dollar clock ticked on the corner shelf. The bath water dripped a little from that loose faucet. She must tell him to tighten it. The roar of the street came up, subdued, even soothing. The heartening smell of something cooking in one of the flats—pot roast, it smelled like.

A key in the lock; the door opened, shut. Wordlessly, in the dim light, he strode to the bed, gathered her in his arms, buried his face in the masses of her damp, fragrant hair.

At half-past six they had a bottle of beer each and a little of the spicy cold ham and one slice of rye bread. Just enough for an appetizer; not enough to spoil their good dinner later on.

The lamp lighted, and the top lights, too, she could see his beloved face. It was the face of a little boy, grown up. The features had never quite crystallized into maturity. A high, rather bulging brow, like a child's. A full mouth, with curling corners, very appealing. Not much chin. Dark curling hair and brown eyes with a hurt look in them because he was a little nearsighted and must not wear glasses. A waiter cannot wear glasses. A weak face, but sweet for a strong woman to look at. She was strong, Fräulein. She had strength and courage and resourcefulness for two.

He was in rebellion, Otto was, against what he called the Capitalistic Class. He was always saying Capitalism must go. The people in the hotel in which he worked were Capitalists, and they must Go. He didn't say where. He took their tips and handed the money over to the thrifty Berta, and said that the Capitalistic Class must Go. Pigs. Slave drivers.

"Of course," Berta agreed. "In two years more, or three, at the most. Carlchen will be four and Camilla six, and they will not need me any more, and we shall

have enough money saved, and we can go back home
and buy the little farm. Oh, Otto! Otto! My darling,
my darling, my darling!"

Well, she must dress.

"How brown you are! Golden, like a little high-yellow
girl from Harlem."

"Yes, isn't it beautiful! Every day, when Carlchen
and Camilla have the sun-lamp I have it, too, longer
than they, because their skin is too delicate. It makes
me strong and healthy, the sun-lamp. And golden all
over. She never takes it. She likes her skin white.
Ugh!"

Arm in arm, very close together, they walked at a
swinging gait down to Eighty-sixth Street in the York-
ville section. The neighborhood was dotted with
restaurants bearing roguish German names—Maxl's;
Drei Mäderl; Brau Stüberl.

Into the warm bright odorous depths of one of these
they popped. Gay checked tablecloths; waiters in
Bavarian peasant garb; round shining faces; music in
which everybody joined. Emil, the *Ober*, was a *Lands-
mann* of Otto. Otto, the waiter, was received by this
head waiter as he himself, in his waiter's uniform,
received a guest of the hated Capitalistic Class. Otto
enjoyed this very much.

He and Berta ordered their dinner. Herring salad,
chicken noodle soup, *Sauerbraten* with potato balls,

apple strudel, coffee. Awaiting this, they buried their faces in enormous foaming steins of beer. They looked at each other across the table. Each reached out for the hand of the other, clasped it a moment, hard; sat back, drank again.

They ate with excellent appetite. Otto had another stein of beer.

Berta shook her head. "Not for me. I don't want to get fat."

"You are just right. I don't like thin."

"Yes. Not thin, like Her, with legs like sticks. But not fat, either. It is not stylish to be fat. Besides, Her good clothes won't fit me if I am not careful."

"Her clothes! You don't need her clothes!" cried Otto, full of class hatred and beer.

"Don't be foolish, Otto darling. Certainly I do. I could not afford to buy anything one tenth as good."

They must go to the Meeting now. Berta was not especially interested in the movement, but Otto was. And the speeches were sometimes interesting, and even exciting. Berta listened and learned and remembered, and held forth, sometimes, to her friends in the park. Otto was a member of a German Nationalistic party with a desire to rule the ruling classes. They set certain dates on which to do it, but it never quite came off. Otto said it would, though, some day, and soon.

The hall was in Eighty-sixth Street, near the East

River. It was crowded and hot and hung with emblems, red muslin, posters of a silly-looking man with a Chaplin mustache, no chin, and one mad and one sane eye. Berta, studying it during the speeches, arrived at this conclusion. She did not speak of it to Otto. The speaker said everything three times.

. . . and so, Comrades, we must give the Worker hands, we must give the Worker feet, we must give the Worker strength . . . until we have the knowledge, until we have the power, until we have the Capital . . . we must prepare for the struggle, we must plan for the struggle, we must be ready for the struggle . . .

But I thought Capital was what they didn't want, Berta thought. It all sounded pretty silly to her, but interesting, too, some of it. It stirred you up. Otto was rapt. His knobby forehead shone. Tiny beads stood on his upper lip. She longed to wipe them away with her handkerchief.

It was ten o'clock. Beer was being served. "Let's go. It is so hot in here. We can go to a movie, for the second show, on Lexington."

They emerged into the clear cold March night. A passing boat hooted hoarsely on the river. The secondary picture was finished, the main picture was not yet started, the weekly news pictures were being shown. They were in luck. Blissfully they sat through the picture, in the warm dark intimacy of the luxurious

seats. Gorgeously dressed and unbelievably slim creatures glided across the screen.

There was music with this picture, sensual and sentimental music. Otto's hand rested on Berta's knee; her
head touched his shoulder. She felt lulled, blissful, a
little sleepy, what with food, love, work, talk, beer,
and the close air.

Five minutes to twelve.

"Otto! Quick! I must take a taxi."

"Oh, what do you care! What can they do? Come
home with me. Please. Darling. *Liebchen.*"

"Don't be foolish, my dearest."

They kissed, there in the bright lights of Lexington
and Eighty-sixth. They clung. This the taxi driver regarded with an urban eye.

"Quick. I am late."

"Where to, lady?"

She reached Sixty-seventh Street not more than
three minutes after twelve. She let herself in quietly,
quietly, but she need not have bothered. The air was
rent, shattered, by the screams from the nursery on the
top floor.

"*Gott!*" She mounted nimbly, spurning the lift.

Lights blazed in the larger room where Fräulein was
wont to sleep with Carlton III, the son, the heir, the
Link. Lights blazed in the smaller adjoining room,
where lay Camilla in the solitary independence of her

adult three years. Fräulein blinked a little, dazedly, what with the lights, and weariness, and the rush up the stairs.

Nancy Schurtz turned, a distraught figure, looking yellow and drawn in her pale blue robe. She turned on a torrent of words above the shrieks of the two infants.

"I thought you'd never come. I can't do anything with them. It's after midnight. We had just got to sleep. The Frasers left at eleven. I was dead. I dreamed that I was riding a horse I used to own, long ago, in Charleston, and I felt myself slipping, and I was under the horse's hoofs and he was trampling me, and neighing in a perfect scream and I woke up and it was Carlton, here, screaming. I had left his nursery door open, of course, because you were out.

"There isn't a thing the matter with him. Not a thing. I've had every stitch off him, and put him on his chair, and he wouldn't. I took his temperature. He hasn't stopped screaming for fifteen minutes. It's sheer devilment, and Camilla, too. I'm worn out. Such a day. They've been fiends. Everything's been horrible. Frederick and Louis had some quarrel, and Frederick gave notice. I'm sure I don't know—and—— Listen to that! I'll spank him, that's what I'll——"

"Go to bed," said Fräulein, calmly. She hung up her coat, went over to the red-faced, howling infant in the blue silk cell. "They will be quiet now." She felt the boy's sleeping garment, wet with sweat. She unbuttoned it, peeled him deftly, wiped him, powdered him, dressed him in a dry garment. She turned out the top lights. His howls abated, and with his, Camilla's. "Go to bed, madam."

The child's arm reached up, the hand rested on her cheek; she turned her head and kissed the soft warm palm. Deep, quivering sighs shook him. Suddenly, miraculously, in that instant, he was asleep. Fräulein made motions with her lips, with her free hand, with her head. They spelled go—go.

Mrs. Carlton Schurtz went back to bed. Carlton Schurtz II opened one fishy gray eye. Whazza?

"Nothing. She's here. They're quieter. Little devils. Poor thing. I wouldn't take her job—not if I were starving. What a life!"

MEADOW LARK
EDNA FERBER

MEADOW LARK

1930

Edna Ferber

MEADOW LARK

WHEN FIRST the winged things had come zooming out
of the sky above the Kansas prairie land old man Trost
used to stand there in the middle of the field he was
plowing—or even when the threshing crew was there—
and shake his great brown fist at them. A stout and
ridiculous Ajax, yet not quite ridiculous, either, in his
impotent wrath, he would turn his face toward the
heavens and utter imprecations in his native tongue.

"*Gott verdammt noch e' mal!*" he would roar. "*Die
Dinger da—die verfluchten Dinger!*" But presently they
became so numerous that the fist-shaking had to be
abandoned. It would have taken too much of his time,
for the government established an airport not four miles
distant from the Trost farm, and glass-roofed airplane
factories glittered like bubbles all over the prairies
skirting the city of Wichita.

Wichita boasted of this, trumpeting: More Airplanes
Made in Wichita Than in Any Other City. But the
Kansas farmers were furious. None so furious, though,

as old man Trost. He threatened to sue the government on the grounds that his farm was being ruined.

The night planes, roaring overhead, disturbed the chickens in their roosts, so that they refused to lay; the stock grew thin with nervousness; the milk dried up in the cows' udders; the mares did not foal, but, maddened by the strange roar always overhead, ramped across the pastures, manes tossing, wild eyes rolling, their hoofs beating a smart tattoo of panic on the fence posts.

Some of that same madness seemed to take hold of old man Trost as the things multiplied—those things swooping and roaring and taunting him from the skies. Here he was, tied to the earth. There they soared, free.

As time went on, the neighboring farmers accepted the new order of things, but Trost never. One of the more daring souls said, "Why don't you take a ride in one? Try it once. Say, you take a look at that farm of yours from five thousand feet up and you'll get a different idea how big it is. It's like you was God and nothing down here is anything. Whole Wichita looks like a toy set for kids."

Trost's face would go mahogany with choler. "If I would get hold once of one of those *verfluchten Dinger* I would show you how it would go up." His brown hands would curve into claws as though he were tearing the soaring thing wing from wing.

Old man Trost was not really old at all; forty-eight

at most. But he had married at eighteen, and his was the settled aspect of one long used to the marital yoke. A powerful man, and dark with a strange darkness belying his Saxon ancestry. A firm barrel of a body, a neck like an ox, short strong legs. A solid-looking man, pot-bellied, burned by the Kansas sun and wind; brusque of speech.

Except for his swarthy coloring he was unromantic of mien; commonplace, almost. A prosperous Midwest farmer, German born, conforming on the surface at least to all the conventional rules for husband, father, citizen. No one knew, no one suspected, that in this unremarkable body rushed the hot blood of the adventurer. Inside, old man Trost was a figure of romance.

Perhaps sometimes Ma Trost wondered about him; but his occasional vagaries she put down to temper or to indigestion. Certainly his temper was something to be reckoned with in that household; a smoldering thing that blazed high and hot into sudden unreasonable rages.

At such times the Trost children, when young, had feared him. When he made for them, arm raised, the scarlet flood of temper turning his brown face to purple, they had scurried for the shelter of their mother's broad haunches and had hidden in the folds of her ample skirts, peering fearfully from this shelter to watch her quelling the storm they had raised.

"Now, Trost, now! Some day by mistake you will hit me, and then you will see. I start for you with the rolling pin like in the movies. Here—get away, all of you—out of my kitchen. *Tapfer, tapfer!*"

His anger would go as quickly as it had come. The brooding darkness, that sat so oddly on this stout farmer, would settle down on him again. Perhaps far, far back in his line a seafaring Spaniard had stayed too well ashore at Hamburg; or an Italian from the north of Italy; or, even more remotely still, a plundering Gaul had come upon a Saxon girl to his fancy.

He had come to America a boy of twelve. The sea had stayed ever in his mind, though he never looked upon it again. The Kansas prairie on which he settled and thrived knew no water except the rain, and even that sometimes withheld itself grudgingly when it was most needed. No one knew that as he plowed the Midwest fields, row on row, the furrows that turned so voluptuously under the plow were waves before the prow of a ship that cut through the green-black waters.

Often enough, in those days of his early youth, one heard of this or that inland farm boy who had run away to sea. He, perhaps, might have been one of them, but the lively girl who now was Ma Trost had caught him and held him fast; and there followed the children, four girls and, last, the boy Theodore; and the Kansas fields to be plowed and planted and added to, acre on acre. They had him now, safe enough from the sea.

The neighboring farmers put him down as odd, this portly man with the big paunch and the bright dark eyes. He grew on his farm things that they never thought of, and would not have attempted if they had.

Strange fowl pecked in his barnyard—birds with odd colorings and haughty struttings. Hens snow-white; roosters like a sunset; speckled things with markings foreign to the common coop. Then he actually attempted to grow peanuts and did, burying them in mounds in a patch of sandy soil and tending them slavishly. They proved little shriveled things at first, but he persisted, and they grew in firmness and plumpness until they were a marvel in this temperate climate.

He planted a vineyard for love of the exotic. With infinite pains and many difficulties he succeeded in perfecting rare varieties—small, sweet, pale green Lady Washingtons; Spanish grapes, purple-black ovals with a down on their dusky cheeks. These he tended in the evening when the others of the family had rattled off to town in the car, to see Laura Lovely in *Passion's Playground.*

He walked alone, softly, in his felt slippers, this burgher, smoking his seasoned pipe; weeding here, spading there, spending in dalliance with his loves the hours that in his thrifty daytime he begrudged them.

His hand, with its thick brown fingers, passed tenderly, lingeringly, over the clustered grapes, like a lover's hand on a woman's breast.

Not one of the children would have dared to eat those grapes unbidden. They sometimes longed to pluck surreptitiously a sweet juicy globe from the under side of a cluster nestling almost hidden in its dark leaves. But they never did. Sometimes—rarely—Ma Trost would cut a whole bunch in a fit of frisky defiance and pass it round as though the green things were emeralds and the blue, sapphires.

Certainly Ma Trost was not the drab farm drudge of fiction. A vast and sprightly woman in a bungalow apron and boudoir cap, with a kind of rich gayety for her husband's dourness. It was she who planted and tended the bright patch of flower garden with its hardy staring blossoms—zinnias, verbenas, asters, blue flag, broad-faced sunflowers.

Even in the winter there stood in the kitchen window a wooden rack holding pots and slips, tier on tier; fuchsias bloomed; there were bleeding heart, geraniums scarlet and pink, bits of cactus. She filled the room with green and growing things and with a kind of hearty abundance; she gave to the house a friendly aspect that offset her husband's dark sullenness; a woman with floury arms, an ample aproned front, little merry eyes that disappeared in wrinkles of laughter.

The four girls had given them a fright, coming like that—one, two, three, four—one after the other. But then, when they were almost despairing, the boy Theodore had come, and everything was all right. In good time the four girls had married readily enough, being healthy, bouncing, red-cheeked creatures with their mother's hearty laugh and her knack with the baking board and kettle. They had gone off with their strapping husbands to near-by farms or to Wichita to live.

Ma Trost saw them often enough, welcomed their growing brood, fed the whole tribe from time to time as they drove up to the Trost farm on Sundays and spilled out of their chunky automobiles. But whether the girls and their families came or went, she had Theodore.

She had Theodore in the house, and she had Theodore there in the near-by fields, but she no more knew Theodore than she knew this dark husband of hers. For while the four girls were fair, the boy was dark like his father, and the two men worked the fields and tended the stock, and both looked up at the darting, droning, winged things high in the sky or swooping impudently close to the Trost housetop and patch of woods.

Try to catch me, you worms down there—you grubs burrowing in the earth. And the dour man of forty-eight looked up and was choked with baffled rage and futility;

but the dark boy of nineteen looked up and his eyes
had the glow, the hope, the resolve of a man who,
gazing at his love as she coquets with him, teases him,
devils him, is serene in the knowledge that this wild
free thing will one day be his, tamed, submissive under
his hand.

To Theo there was nothing new or strange about
these flying things as there was to an older generation.
He had seen them and heard them since early childhood.
They were an accepted fact—as much a part of the
order of things as the automobile, the telephone, the
phonograph. He loved all things motor-driven, but this
thing he worshiped. It not only moved; it flew, spurning
the ground. It was more than a motor, more than a ship.
An air ship.

"Stop reading them magazines once and go like the
other boys," Ma Trost was forever saying. Or, "You
ain't going to work again in that shed, tinkering all
hours of the night! Why'n't you take Bertha to the
movie in town? How she sits there in the evening with
her pa, that poor girl, with her education and all, so
smart, and pretty, too, Bertha Muller is. H'm? Why
don't you, once, Theo?"

He would glance absently up at her from the magazine he was reading or the bench at which he was
working.

The magazines were always the same—*Mechanical*

Age; Air; Motor; The Pilot; Aviation. Their ads said:
Are You Hungry for Popularity, Adventure, Big Pay?
Then Choose Aviation.

Are You a Red-Blooded, Daring He-Man?

A picture accompanying this of a helmeted Lind-
berghian youth.

He had made for himself a workshop in an old shed
that had been an abandoned henroost. Little by little,
painfully, with the dimes, quarters, and half-dollars that
came his way in that thrifty German farm household—
the small change that other lads of his age spent for
movies, soft drinks, girls, fancy shirts—he had acquired
tools, a motor, all the necessities of a workshop.

Before he was sixteen he had practically built for
himself an automobile out of such odds and ends as
only a born mechanic could assemble and invest magically with the power of locomotion. Shivering, snarling,
rattling in every bolt and screw, it still could miraculously outdistance the plump middle-class family car.

Ma Trost would trot out to the shed after their early
supper and stand in the doorway, surveying her last-
born with a mingled pride and impatience. "Such a
grand girl, poor Bertha, and there she sits on a lovely
evening like this with her sick pa."

At her importuning he glanced up abstractedly. He
had the clear childlike eyes, the wise guileless face of
the natural mechanic—of one to whom a motor is a

more living thing than a human being. Sweetness was there, and strength and utter detachment.

"Leave her sit."

It was not that he disliked the Muller girl. He liked her well enough. He did not love her. Perhaps he realized, vaguely, that the Muller girl and Ma Trost were conspiring to take from him his real love—his real love with whom he spent every evening far into the night, and who was in his thoughts all through the long bright day.

The thought of her was all that sustained him during the day as he plowed and sowed and garnered under the Kansas sun. An exquisite thing, his love, frail, yet strong; slim, vibrant, infinitely exciting; all steel and light, light spruce wood, and cotton. Sometimes, when he thought of her, the blood ebbed from his heart and rushed into his head, almost blinding him, suffocating him, then surged back again to his heart so that he thought it would burst.

The Bertha Muller girl indeed!

Sometimes he saw her and even took her to the pictures or to a picnic. He liked being with her, in a vague, remote sort of way. She let him kiss her once or twice, primly, and he had rather enjoyed that. She was a good girl, the Muller girl, and smart. Ma Trost kept dinning that into his ears. Not like those other girls, running around Wichita all the time, in silk stockings

and skirts to their knees and high heels, and no more
know how to cook or keep house than *Gott weiss was.*

She had gone to the normal school at Emporia, and
after that had taught for a whole year at good pay.
Then, in one year, her mother had died, her father had
suffered a stroke, and there was the rich Muller farm
to be worked by strangers, with Bertha called home to
act as housekeeper and nurse.

Old Muller could whirl himself about in a wheel chair
now, and the Wichita doctor promised that in another
year perhaps he could walk. But the Muller farm, with
its bountiful acres, needed a guiding hand. Bertha's
husband was the man for the place. But Bertha had no
husband, though a few came wooing.

It was surprising that more did not come, for she was
comely enough, strong, capable. They seemed to prefer
the new order of farm girl—the flutter-budget of whom
Ma Trost spoke with such contempt. Bertha Muller
frightened them with her serious face, her determined
mien, her bossy ways, her manner of coming down hard
on her heels, as though to crush something underfoot.
They were troubled to explain it, these inarticulate
Kansas farm swains.

"It's like she was teacher all the time, and you was
pupil and she caught you throwing spitballs."

Still, she could have married one of them, and would
have; but the Muller girl, so strong, so independent,

was in love with Trosts' Theodore, who looked at her with the eyes of one who sees through her and beyond her, to something far distant and dear.

Airplanes. Airplanes. Always reading and studying about those crazy airplanes. She and Ma Trost put their heads together. Theirs was a silent understanding. They would tame this meadow lark, and cage him.

They did not say to each other: We will tame him. We will sprinkle crumbs on the doorsill and he will be afraid at first, but he will hop nearer and nearer, though at the slightest sound he will fly away. But pretty soon he will not be afraid, and he will come every day to eat, and then one day we will reach down softly, softly—and have him, and hold him.

"Bertha invited us to dinner Sunday, Pa and me and you. It will be nice I don't have to cook a big dinner once on Sunday."

"I don't want to go."

"Theo, what is got into you? That poor Bertha, she fixes all week we should come to dinner on Sunday and cheer her pa up a little. I guess you can do that much for somebody that has got trouble and not always have to sit in that shed with your face full of grease from a engine, and your clothes. It's bad enough to wash farm clothes clean without your dirty engine clothes that the grease won't come out at all."

He went sulkily. The Muller girl received them, and

it was as though she were panting with a breathless energy. She went back and forth between stove and table, though they had a hired girl.

Bertha's cheeks were pink with the heat and excitement. There were tiny beads of moisture on her upper lip and her temples and in the cleft of her firm round chin. She had the short sturdy fibula of the energetic woman and seemed to take more steps and to come down harder than was absolutely necessary.

"My, this is good!" chanted Ma Trost, over and over. "My, Bertha, did you cook this all yourself?"

"Every bite." Her firm cheeks flushed pinker. She glanced at Theo. His eyes were on his plate.

"Well, I thought I was a cook, but I guess you make me take a back seat, all right. Dumplings I can never get light like this. Some man is going to be lucky some day."

"Oh, now, Mrs. Trost!"

"Pa Trost will be complaining about how I fix his eating after this, with mayonnaise and whipped cream and puff paste and such little finger rolls and what."

"You cook good enough for me," Pa Trost muttered, somberly. Both he and Theo had pushed the golden crown of mayonnaise off their unaccustomed salad with an investigating fork, had looked down at the mixed fruit mass beneath and had sat back with the mien of the male who disdains feminized food.

The paralytic, silent through most of the meal, at this unfortunate moment piped up in his reedy voice.

"Now'days boys don't marry girls because they can cook, like when I was young. They would sooner eat out of a tin can and a paper bag from the delicatessen in Wichita if she is got a cute shape and can switch her hips around when she walks."

Pink deepened to red in the Muller girl's cheeks.

Mrs. Trost bridled. "I'm surprised, Mr. Muller, how you can talk like that in front of Bertha here and Theo."

The boy, hearing his name, looked up. "What?"

"Mr. Muller, talking like that."

"I didn't hear him," said Theo.

What could you do with a boy like that?

Bertha tried the wiles of those other girls—the new farm girls of the district with their bobbed hair and small close hats and silk stockings and silk dresses bought out of the window of the department store in Wichita. She knew. Those other boys who had come courting Bertha had pressed against her meaningly with a knee, a thigh, a hard-muscled arm or shoulder. So now, on those rare occasions when she rode with him in his quivering car, or walked down the road with him and sat with him a moment in his work shed as she visited the Trost farm on some flimsy neighborly pretext, she experimented, using age-old instinct as her guide.

Goaded, doubtless, by Ma Trost, Theo had driven Bertha into town one evening in late May. They had seen a picture. They had had an ice-cream soda at the drugstore counter. Now they were driving back to the farm in Theo's homemade and feverish car. Its whole frame was shaken as by a palsy when you started its engine, but it leaped like the mad thing it was, once set going.

The Kansas sky hung low. From the east a crouching storm, about to spring, showed its fangs from time to time, and growled in warning. As they rattled along the road they passed the signal lights that marked the aviator's course toward the landing field. It was well past eleven o'clock.

"Let's us go out to the field and see the mail plane come in, huh?"

"Oo, it's going to storm. Look. And anyway, it's late."

"That's anyway a half an hour off, that storm. I can tell. Come on. Let's."

"Well—all right, Theo."

As the generations before them, craving adventure even at second hand, had lounged down to the railway depot to watch Number Nine or Number Twelve rush, panting, into the town and out again, coming from strange lands east and bound for unseen plains west, so now these of the newest adult generation achieved a vicarious thrill from the arrival and departure of that traveler of the air—the midnight mail plane.

Bertha Muller inched her way cautiously toward him as he sat so quiet, so quiet and remote, at the wheel of his crazy car. She had known the warm prickling thrill that had come when those others had met her in momentary contact—those other boys of her virginal experience; hearty fellows, strong, with the good hard flesh on them from manual labor and the plain plentiful food of the region—bread, pies, pork, mashed potatoes, beans, gravy. So she pressed against him a little as they sat there side by side—not boldly, but hopefully, askingly—a warm touch of the knee, the soft hip, the shoulder. But when she pressed against him like that it was like pressing against steel, so hard he was, so unyielding, so unresponsive.

She, too, fell silent a moment. Nothing. Well, she would try another tack.

"I always think," she began, in her prim normal-school accents, "how wonderful it is that we should be driving along like this, farmer folks that we are. Here we have been into town and seen a movie, and are coming back and going to see the night plane come in, and all. Electricity on the farms, and all kinds of modern inventions.

"We don't have to work like your ma and pa did, and mine. That's all past, that kind of slaving on a farm.

When I think of my folks. My mother never had any fun in her life—anyway, not after she married. But now'days farming is fun, really.

"I would be perfectly happy on the farm, really. I used to miss my teaching, and the—uh—mental contacts I had. If I only had somebody to help me, and advise, and look to. Papa won't live long. I might as well face that, because it's coming, and you have to face the facts of life. And then I will be left all alone, with that big valuable farm on my hands—a woman, alone."

"Yeh," said Theo. "That's tough."

She gave an impatient movement, then controlled herself, relaxed again, patient, patient. "I suppose I could get married to one of the boys that's always hanging around. But I'm not the kind of a girl that would marry just to have a man on my farm. My, no!"

"Good a reason as any," said Theo, and stepped on the gas. They shot into the parking space behind the low shed that marked the landing field.

There was always a gathering of people on the field on warm summer nights, to watch the midnight mail plane come in. Something of mystery still was in it, and romance, and daring, even to this community accustomed to the wheeling, whirring, swooping things in the sky above their farms and houses. People drove out from Wichita itself.

The shed was warmly lighted, and stifling. Outside stood little scattered groups. The landing-field light went off, and on, and off, and on, a Cyclops eye turned toward the sky. But the gravel-covered landing field itself was flooded with a strong white light, made more unreal and blinding because of the brooding darkness just beyond.

The sky now was low and black and ominous. The jagged thrusts were more venomous, more frequent, and the growl more urgent.

"He better step on it if he's going to make it," the onlookers said, peering into the blackness. Women's figures in light summer dresses. Men smoking and looking up at the sky. Their faces were strangely pure, raised like that to the heavens, with something of wonder in them, and expectation.

A tiny light, closer and closer, out of the east. "Here she comes."

A man ran out of the shed, shooing the crowd back to safety. Keep away, folks. Keep clear. Don't want to get hurt. Get back, now.

Nearer, nearer. A movement of panic; a darting back to safety. The incredible thing swooped down out of the air, came scuttling along the field scattering dust and gravel in a cloud as it came to a stop.

A lean young figure in corduroy and leather slung a lank leg over the cockpit. He unstrapped from about his waist a clumsy-looking contraption that the wise knew to be his parachute. His shoulders, in the limp blue shirt, slumped. He walked stiffly toward the shed.

"Hello, Fred."

"'Lo, Otto."

"How's she blowing?"

"Pretty good. Guess I can make Denver before she hits me. Got to step on it, though."

The crowd closed about the birdlike thing curiously, as though they were seeing its like for the first time. Inside the shed the boy in the blue shirt made his report, deposited his sack, gathered up the west-bound mail. He emerged again, quickly, with a final bite of ham sandwich bulging his cheek.

He wiped his mouth with the back of his hard palm, climbed into the cockpit, was off, with another scattering of gravel and dust, another backward surge from the crowd. Off. Up, up. Higher. The growling, flashing animal was close behind him now, leaping just behind him from the east, showing its fangs like a ravenous thing. The tail light suddenly turned. He was coming back.

He encircled the field once, in farewell. Showing off. The crowd, sensing this, laughed with a kind of excited admiration, such as they would give a lion tamer who plays with the ferocious animal in its cage at the circus. The tail light grew smaller, dimmer, winked once, vanished into the high blackness.

The crowd gave a sigh, deep, as though awakened from a dream. They stumbled a little as they walked toward their waiting cars.

Theo and Bertha climbed into their little car, were off with a shiver and a leap. A tight cold band of steel was tightening around the girl's heart. She laughed in mirthless pretense of laughter.

"Well, I'd rather it would be him than me," she quavered, forgetting her normal-school training. "I'll take my farm and my nice safe bed, thank you."

The boy said nothing. Absolutely nothing. If he had protested; if only he had sneered at her fear, or laughed at her, or defended this lean sky god in the soiled blue shirt. But he said nothing, sitting there, tight-lipped, at the wheel.

But he was, after all, human and male. And here was a woman—admiring, wondering—in whom to confide the secret of his strength. So, a scant quarter of a mile before they reached her farmyard, this young Samson confided in his Delilah.

"I'll be up in a day or two."

"Up?"

"Don't you let on to my folks. Pa and Ma, they don't understand. I been making a plane. I been a year at it. That's why I come out tonight. I wanted to get away from her for one evening, to get fresh, so I could look her over tomorrow with new eyes. She's in the lean-to, behind my work shed. Nobody knows but you. I kept that door locked. Day after tomorrow I knock out the whole side of the lean-to, and trundle her out, and up in her at sunset, after supper."

"But Theo, how do you know—maybe it isn't right or something—what if you fall? Oh, Theo, your ma—you ought to tell your ma, anyway."

"That's right. Go on and blab."

"I won't. I won't."

But he left her angrily at the gate, not troubling to get out of the car to help her. He was off, the thing snarling and chattering down the road in a fury of anger against her, against all womankind. She stood there, in the farm gateway. The rain came; great pelting drops, heavy, like warm lead.

He seemed to sense that in her love for him he could not trust her. She cared more for his bones than her honor.

Next evening, after supper, she left the sick man and was down the road in her own car toward the Trost farm. She drove swiftly and well, her strong brown hands capable at the wheel.

Ma Trost was watering her flowers. Pa Trost, in his slippers and shirt sleeves, was smoking an after-supper pipe in the cool of the kitchen doorway.

"Hello," called Bertha, very casual. "Hello. Where's Theo?"

"Hello, Bertha. How's your pa?"

"All right. He's all right. Where's Theo?"

Ma Trost laughed her hearty laugh that shook her vast bosom. "In that shed of his, tinkering. Go back, once, and talk to him. My, you look cute in that pink dress. Don't she, Pa? Like a rose."

From the shed came the sound of hammering, loud on the still evening air. Hammering, and boards being rent from their nailings. A sudden premonition seized Bertha Muller. Her whole body stiffened as she stood there. The hammering ceased. A whirring sound then, loud, loud, louder. Her pink cheeks went putty-colored.

"Come!" she screamed suddenly, like a madwoman. "Come. Quick. It's Theo. He's going up."

She began to run. The man and the woman stared at her a moment. Then they, too, began to run toward the roaring, whirring sound, clumsily, heavily. They looked ridiculous, running like that, the fat woman in her apron, the paunchy man with his pipe.

The thing, awkward yet fleet and somehow graceful in its awkwardness, careened across the open field as they reached the ruined lean-to. A tiny winged thing, almost moth-like against the green of the field.

Across the field it went, into the meadow beyond, wheeled, turned, came toward them, so that they ran back fearfully; turned again, made off at higher speed, wheeled, turned, again and again and again and again, so that the three standing there in an agony of fear and suspense finally realized that this winged thing was tied to the earth—that its wings were powerless to lift it. Again it came toward them, turned, made off, turned, raced back. Stopped.

Theo stepped out of the tiny cockpit. His face was set and terrible. He looked at the man and the woman and the girl. He seemed not to see them.

"She won't lift," he said simply. Then, suddenly, in a louder voice, "She won't lift." His set expression broke, then, in a grimace of sickening disappointment and impotent rage, so that the three involuntarily turned their eyes away, ashamed to look upon his agony.

Ma Trost went toward him then. "Oh, Theo, what do you—how you can scare me like that?"

"Leave me alone. Leave me alone. She won't lift. She's no good. God damn it! She's no good." He began to cry—the horrible crying of a man betrayed by the thing he loves.

Here was a situation for Pa Trost's handling. He advanced on the boy, his face darker than was its wont. His great hands were clenched into fists. "You try to go up in one of them things again I break every bone in your body. You hear me! I smash it into a thousand pieces, that *Gott verdammte Ding!*"

Theodore picked up a hammer from the ground near the work shed. He raised it high, threateningly. "You touch it and I'll break your head. Yes, you!"

Then, as his father stood, open-mouthed, purple with rage and astonishment, the boy swung the hammer back and brought it down on the wings of the frail light craft—down, and up, and down and up and down and up, until the white cotton stuff, so strong, so flimsy, fluttered in ribbons.

"Oh, Theo!" whimpered Bertha Muller; and covered her face with her hands.

The boy threw the hammer far away into the field. He faced them then, set and stern. His hysteria was past. "Look," he said. "I'm going to the factory. I'm through."

"Through!" echoed Ma Trost feebly. "What— through?"

"I'm through farming, see? I'm going to get a job in the factory and learn to make planes right, not like that piece of junk. And fly. I'm going to fly a mail plane yet. You'll see."

Pa Trost again. "You crazy, you! You crazy! You stay here on the farm and work, you fool, you. I've got enough now of this airplanes. You with your airplane, it won't even go one inch off the muck in the field. A fine airplane flyer you are. You go in the house now, and first you take that junk and kindling and old rags off of my good field. I show you who is a flyer in this house. I make you fly, all right, with my foot behind you."

"Good-bye," said the boy. He walked past them.

"Theo, where are you going?"

"You come back here, *du Narr du! Du—du Verrück-ter!* You stay here or I make you."

"Yeh? How you going to make me stay? Put me in jail!"

The Eagle Aircraft Company's plant had, curiously, the brilliant airy look of a huge playroom. It was all windows, or almost all, so that the golden Kansas sun shone on steel and wire and on pieces of wood that were broad and thick, and yet light as a feather when you lifted them. Spruce, or balsa from South America, weighing no more than paper.

You saw other boys there, like Theo, with the look of the farm still on them; corn-colored hair, cornflower-blue eyes, working patiently at this or that menial task, the brimless crown of an old straw hat atop their heads as they worked. They dreamed of the clouds as they worked, but they worked carefully, none the less. Large printed signs were tacked up here, there, everywhere.

REPORT ALL MISTAKES IMMEDIATELY. FAILURE TO DO SO MAY MEAN THE DEATH OF A BRAVE MAN.

They set him to mopping floors, this farm boy who had been the pet of the woman-ridden household, the apple of his mother's eyes. And he scrubbed them. He was farther from flying than he ever had been in his work-shed days on the farm. They wouldn't let him go near a plane, or scarcely.

Theo come home your pa will forgive you you are breaking my hart your ma.

Bertha wrote, too, in her firm round hand:

Dear Theodore, I am writing to you, though you haven't written a word to poor me, because I think somebody ought to tell you how your mother is grieving, and your father too, though he doesn't let on. I think you ought to remember that they are old people now, and that we young people ought to make life happier and easier for them . . .

He answered his mother briefly; Bertha, too.

When you see me flying over the farm you'll know I am willing to come home. But not to stay home. I will let you know.

They paid him an infinitesimal wage, and he pulled in his belt and lived on it. Sometimes, at night—and in the daytime, too—he dreamed of the bountiful steaming noonboard that Ma Trost had always spread.

He was a natural mechanic and a natural flyer. Born in the age of flying, in the region where flying was thickest, it was as inevitable that he should one day learn to fly, and fly always thereafter, as that another should learn to walk.

He picked up the trade slang and work phrases readily enough. He learned to call the cockpit the "office." Aileron. Dural. Dope. The three types of plane that stood all about the huge bright room in every stage, from the metal skeleton to the completed ship, had, for him, the definite personalities of so many human beings.

The mail plane, big, substantial, businesslike, dependable, a thing built to stand the daily grind, summer and winter, in all kinds of weather. The sport plane, like a pretty, frivolous girl, made for pleasure—a butterfly thing, white and scarlet and gay. The army plane, gray, grim, sinister.

One day they let him hand things to a friendly pilot. Weeks passed. One day they let him clean a spark plug. Weeks passed. He got a ride now and again, and was silent. He had a feel for the air as a born automobile racer has a feel for the road.

One day a silent, good-natured pilot took him up and in a burst of generosity let him have the controls for one moment, when they were high enough to be safe. Theo took them, his young face stern. The pilot watched him narrowly, though he appeared casual enough. Once he had been up with a kid who froze to the sticks, and he had barely had time to hammer and wrench the kid's fingers loose and grab the controls himself, and right her.

Six months. Ten. A year. Ma Trost had driven out to see him, of course, many times, and had brought him baskets, napkin-covered. Bertha Muller, too. But always his face had set in those lines of resolve. Pa Trost never came.

The Trost telephone rang at half-past five on a June night, as Ma Trost was getting the supper. Her hearty chuckling laugh was heard less often these days.

A mysterious voice over the telephone. A voice strange to her. "Tonight at half-past six over the farm three times."

"What?" shrieked Ma Trost, who always talked too loudly on the telephone. "What you say?"

"Tonight at half-past six over the farm three times. Watch the sky."

"What?"

But the voice had gone.

She knew. She telephoned Bertha then. She tried to get Theodore at the airplane factory, but there was no answer; at his boarding house. He was not there.

Bertha arrived, white and shaking. "Did you tell Pa Trost?"

"No. I don't know should I."

"I wouldn't. Call him out. No—you'd better tell him first."

She told him. Half-past six, over the farm. Three times. He said nothing.

Pa Trost ate his supper as usual; silent, somber. Ma Trost ate nothing. Bertha explained that she had had her supper early. The two women listened. The man pretended not to.

The two women went to the back porch and stood there, in the June evening light. The man stayed within. The smell of his pipe drifted out to them.

They heard the humming, the buzzing, the roaring before they saw it.

Their sharp eyes, accustomed to distances, saw him then, a speck, a tiny winged thing like a meadow lark high up in the evening sky. Then it came lower, lower still.

"That's him," said Bertha simply. "Here. Do you want the glasses?" She had brought binoculars with her.

"I don't need no glasses . . . Pa! Pa, come out. It's Theo. Up there."

They stood, their faces raised to the sky. It circled the farm once. It circled the farm twice. Old man Trost drew a deep breath, like a sob, and his face went the color of dark red wine. He shook his fist in the air, a gesture of futility and bafflement. Then he turned, walking heavily in his soft felt slippers, and went into the house and shut the door with a violence that caused the two women watchers to start and cry out.

Three times. And now the graceful, whirring, wheeling thing dipped, swooped, banked, spiraled. Ma Trost covered her face with her shaking hand. Then, fascinated, she must look up again. Her left hand, with the broad gold band deeply embedded in the flesh of the fourth finger, pleated and unpleated her kitchen apron in an agony of terror.

"I'm afraid for him. Look how he makes! I'm afraid he is killed. I'm afraid he drops down in the field, and is killed."

The winged thing, its third circle completed, darted off now toward the west.

Bertha Muller lowered her binoculars slowly. She looked, suddenly, old. Her voice, when she spoke, was hard and without life.

"Don't you worry. He won't come down. He won't —ever come down."

HEY! TAXI!

EDNA FERBER

HEY! TAXI!

1928

Edna Ferber

HEY! TAXI!

Nervous old ladies from Dubuque, peering fearfully at the placard confronting them as they rode in Ernie's taxi, waxed more timorous still as they read it. It conveyed a grisly warning. Attached thereto was a full-face photograph of Ernie. Upon viewing this, their appraising glance invariably leaped, startled, to where Ernie himself loomed before them in the driver's seat on the other side of the glass partition. Immediately there swept over them an impulse to act upon the printed instructions.

POLICE DEPARTMENT
CITY OF NEW YORK

Ernest Stewig

This is a photograph of the authorized driver.
If another person is driving this cab notify a policeman.

Staring limpidly back at one from the official photograph was a sleek, personable, and bland young man. This Ernest Stewig who basked in police approval was modishly attired in a starched white collar, store clothes, and a not too rakish fedora. His gaze met yours frankly, and yet with a certain appeal. Trust me, it said.

From a survey of this alleged likeness the baffled eye swung, fascinated, to the corporeal and workaday Ernie seated just ahead, so clearly outlined against the intervening glass.

A pair of pugnacious red ears outstanding beneath a checked gray and black cap well pulled down over the head; a soft blue shirt, somewhat faded; or, in winter, a maroon sweater above whose roll rose a powerful and seemingly immovable neck. Somewhere between the defiant ears and the monolithic neck you sensed a jaw to which a photograph could have done justice only in profile. You further felt that situate between the cap's visor and the jaw was a pair of eyes before which the seraphic gaze of the pictured Ernie would have quailed. The head never moved, never turned to right or left; yet its vision seemed to encompass everything. It was like a lighthouse tower, regnant, impregnable, raking the maelstrom below with a coldly luminous scrutiny.

About the whole figure there was something panther-like—a quietly alert, formidable, and almost sinister quality—to convey which was in itself no mean achievement for a young man slouched at the wheel of a palpably repainted New York taxicab.

Stewig. Stewig! The name, too, held a degree of

puzzlement. The passenger's brain, rejecting the eye's message, sent back a query: Stewig? Isn't there a consonant missing?

Just here the n. o. l. from Dubuque had been known to tap on the glass with an apprehensive but determined forefinger.

"Young man! Young man! Is this your taxicab you're driving?"

"What's that?"

"I said, are you driving this taxi?"

"Well, who'd you think was driving it, lady?"

"I mean are you the same young man as in the picture here?"

Then Ernie, to the horror of his fare, might thrust his head in at the half-open window, unmindful of the traffic that swirled and eddied all about him.

"Me? No. I'm a couple of other guys," and smile.

In spite of sweater, cap, jaw, ears, and general bearing, when Ernie smiled you recognized in him the engaging and highly sartorial Ernest Stewig photographically approved by the local constabulary. Apologetic and reassured, the passenger would relax against the worn leather cushion.

About Ernie there was much that neither police nor passenger knew. About police and passenger there was little that Ernie did not know. And New York was the palm of his hand. Not only was Ernie the authorized driver of this car; he was its owner. He had bought it second-hand for four hundred dollars. Its four cylinders made rhythmic music in his ears. He fed it oil, gas, and water as a mother feeds her babe. He was a member in good standing of the United Taxi Men's Association. He belonged to Mickey Dolan's Democratic Club for reasons more politic than political.

In his left coat pocket he carried the gray-bound booklet which was his hack-driver's license—a tiny telltale pamphlet of perhaps a dozen pages. At the top of each left-hand page was printed the word VIOLATION. At the top of each right-hand page was the word DISPOSITION. If, during the year, Ernie had been up for speeding; for parking where he shouldn't; for wearing his hackman's badge on his left lapel instead of his right; for any one of those myriad petty misdemeanors which swarm like insects above a hackman's head, that small crime now would appear inevitably on the left-hand page, as would his punishment therefor on the right-hand.

Here it was, November. The pages of Ernie's little gray book were virgin.

It must not be assumed that this was entirely due to the high moral plane on which Ernie and his four-cylinder second-hand cab (repainted) moved. He was careful, wise, crafty, and almost diabolically gifted at the wheel. When you rode with Ernie you got there—

two new gray hairs, perhaps, and the eye pupils slightly
dilated—but you got there. His was a gorgeous and
uncanny sense of timing. You turned the green-light
corner just one second before the sanguine glare of the
Stop light got you. Men passengers of his own age,
thirtyish, seemed to recognize a certain quality in his
manipulation of the wheel. They said, "What outfit
were you with?"

There were many like him penduluming up and down
the narrow tongue of land between the Hudson and the
East River. He was of his day: hard, tough, disillusioned,
vital and engaging. He and his kind had a pitying
contempt for those grizzled, red-faced old fellows whose
hands at the wheel were not those of the mechanic,
quick, deft, flexible, but those of the horseman, bred
to the reins instead of the steering gear. These drove
cautiously, their high-colored faces set in anxiety, their
arms stiffly held. Theirs were rattling old cars for which
they had no affection and some distrust. They sat in
the driver's seat as though an invisible rug were tucked
about their inflexible knees. In their eyes was an expectant look—imploring, almost—as though they hoped
the greasy engine would turn somehow, magically, into
a quadruped. Past these Ernie's car flashed derisively.

"How's hackin', old-timer?"

Up and down, up and down the little Island he raced.
New York swore at him, growled at him, confided in

him, overtipped him, undertipped him, borrowed money from him, cheated him, rewarded him, bribed him, invited him to crime. His knowledge of New York was fearful. He forever was talking of leaving it. He complained of the dullness of business, of the dullness of life. He never talked to you unless you first talked to him, after which you had some difficulty in shutting him up. He had a sweet, true, slightly nasal tenor which he sometimes obligingly loaned to college boys with a yen for harmonizing while on a bust. His vocabulary in daily use consisted of, perhaps, not more than two hundred words. He was married. He was fond of his wife, Josie. His ambition, confided under the slightest encouragement, was to open a little country hotel, with a bar, somewhere up the river, with a quiet but brisk bootlegging business on the side. To this end he worked fifteen hours a day; toward it he and Josie saved his money. It was their idyll.

"Yeh, hackin', there's nothing in it. Too many cabs, see? And overhead! Sweet je's, lookit. Insurance thirty bucks a month and you got to pay it. If you ain't got your sticker every month—yeh, that's it—that blue paper on the windshield, see?—you're drove off the street by the cops and you get a ticket. Sure. You gotta insure. Garage, twenty-five. Paint your car once a year anyway is fifty. Oil and gas, two-fifty a day. Five tires a year, and a good shoe sets you back twenty-eight fifty.

That says nothing about parts and repairs. Where are you, with anyway fifteen hunnerd a year and nearer two grand? No, I only got just this one hack. No, I wouldn't want no jockey. I drive it alone. They don't play square with you, see? It ain't worth the worry of an extra bus. Yeh, I see aplenty and hear aplenty. Keep your eyes and ears open in the hackin' game, and your mouth shut, and you won't never get into a jam is the way I figger."

Strange fragments of talk floated out to Ernie as he sat so stolidly there at the wheel, looking straight ahead:

"Don't! There! I've lost an earring."

"—five dollars a quart——"

"—sick and tired of your damn nagging——"

"—you do trust me, don't you, babe?"

Up and down, up and down, putting a feverish city to bed. Like a racked and restless patient who tosses and turns and moans and whimpers, the town made all sorts of notional demands before finally it composed its hot limbs to fitful sleep.

Light! cried the patient. Light!

All right, said Ernie. And made for Broadway at Times Square.

I want a drink! I want a drink!

Sure, said Ernie. And stopped at a basement door with a little slit in it and an eye on the other side of the slit.

I want something to eat!

Right, said Ernie. And drove to a place whose doors never close and whose windows are plethoric with roast turkeys, jumbo olives, cheeses, and sugared hams.

It's hot! It's hot! I want to cool off before I go to sleep!

Ernie trundled his patient through the dim aisles of Central Park and up past the midnight velvet of Riverside Drive.

One thing more. Under his seat, just behind his heels and covered by the innocent roll of his raincoat, Ernie carried a venomous fourteen-inch section of cold, black, solid iron pipe. Its thickness was such that the hand could grasp it comfortably and quickly. A jack handle, it was called affectionately.

Though he affected to be bored by his trade he deceived no one by his complaints; not even himself. Its infinite variety held him; its chanciness; the unlimited possibilities of his day's vagaries. Josie felt this. Josie said, "You'll be hackin' when you're sixty and so stiff-knuckled your fingers can't wrap around the wheel."

"Sixty, I'll be pushing you in a wheel chair if you don't take off some that suet."

They loved each other.

Saturday. Any day in Ernie's life as a hackman might bring forth almost anything, and frequently did. But Saturday was sure to. Saturday, in winter, was a long hard day and night and Ernie awoke to it always much as a schoolboy contemplates his Saturday, bright and new-minted. It held all sorts of delightful possibilities.

Saturday, in late November. Having got in at 4 A. M., he awoke at noon, refreshed.

Josie had been up since eight. She did not keep hackman's hours. Josie's was a rather lonely life. She complained sometimes, but not often; just enough to keep Ernie interested and a little anxious. A plump neat woman with slim, quick ankles; deep-bosomed; a careful water-wave; an excellent natural cook; she dressed well and quietly, eschewing beige with a wisdom that few plump women have. Ernie took pride in seeing her smartly turned out on their rare holidays together. A lonely and perforce an idle wife, she frequented the movies both afternoon and evening, finding in their shadowy love-making and lavishness a vicarious thrill and some solace during Ernie's long absences.

His breakfast was always the same. Fruit, toast, coffee—the light breakfast of a man who has had his morning appetite ruined by a late lunch bolted before going to bed. Josie had eaten four hours earlier. She lunched companionably with him as he breakfasted. It was, usually, their only meal together. As she prepared it, moving deftly about the little kitchen in her print dress and a terrible boudoir cap, Ernie went up on the roof, as was his wont, to survey the world and to fool for five minutes with Big Bum, the family police dog, named after Ernie's pet aversion, the night traffic cop at the corner of Forty-fifth and Broadway. He it was who made life hard for hackmen between the hours of nine-thirty and eleven, when they were jockeying for the theater break.

The Stewigs' flat was one of the many brownstone walk-ups in West Sixty-fifth Street; a sordid and reasonably respectable row of five-story ugliness whose roofs bristled with a sapling forest of radio aërials. A little rickety flight of stairs and a tiny tar-papered shed led to an exhilarating and unexpected view of sky and other low-lying roofs, and a glimpse of the pocket-edition Statue of Liberty on top of the Liberty Storage Warehouse, and even a bit of the Hudson if you leaned over the parapet and screwed your neck around.

Ernie liked it up there. It gave him a large sense of freedom, of dominance. He and Big Bum tussled and bounded and rolled about a bit within the narrow confines of their roof world. They surveyed the western hemisphere. Big Bum slavered and pawed and bowed and scraped his paws and wagged his tail and shimmied his flanks and went through all the flattering and sycophantic attitudes of the adoring canine who craves masculine company, being surfeited with feminine.

"Ernie!" a voice up the airshaft. "Coffee's getting cold!"

Big Bum threw his whole heart into his effort to hold his master on the roof. He bared his fangs; growled; set his forefeet menacingly. Ernie slapped him on the rump, tousled his muzzle, tickled his stomach with a fond toe. "Come on, Bum."

"Aw, no!" said Bum, with his eyes. "Let's not pay any attention to her. Couple of men like us."

"Ernie! Don't beef to me if your toast is leather."

"Come on, Bum." Down they went to domesticity.

"What time'll you be home, do you think?"

"How should I know?"

"You couldn't stop by for dinner, could you, late? Nice little steak for you, maybe, or a pork tenderloin and lemon pie?"

"On a Saturday? You're cuckoo!"

"Well, I just thought."

"Yeh! Don't go bragging."

They had discussed a child in rare conjugal moments. "Wait," Ernie had said, "till we got the place up the river with a back yard for the kid like I had time I was little and lived in Jersey, and he can fool with Bum and like that. Here, where'd he be but out on the street being run over?"

"Yes," said Josie, not too delicately. "Let's wait till I'm fifty."

She bade him good-bye now, somewhat listlessly.

"Well, anyway, you're not working tomorrow, are you, Ernie? Sunday?"

"No. Give the other guy a chance tomorrow. We'll go somewheres."

They did not kiss one another good-bye. After seven years of marriage they would have considered such daytime demonstration queer, not to say offensive.

One o'clock. Over to the garage on Sixty-ninth for the hack. Gas, oil, and water. These services he himself performed, one of the few taxi men to whom the engine of a car was not as mysterious and unexplored as the heavenly constellations. It was a saying among hackmen that most of them did not know what to do when the engine was boiling over. Ernie's car had been cleaned during the morning. Still, he now extracted from beneath the seat cushion a flannel rag with which he briskly rubbed such metal parts as were, in his opinion, not sufficiently resplendent.

He had fitted the car with certain devices of his own of which he was extremely proud. Attached to the dashboard, at the right, was a little metal clip which held his pencil. Just below the meter box hung a change slot such as street-car conductors wear. It held dimes, quarters, and nickels and saved Ernie much grubbing about in coat pockets while passengers waited, grumbling.

Out through the broad, open door of the garage and

into the lemon-yellow sunshine of a sharp November Saturday. A vague nostalgia possessed him momentarily. Perhaps they were burning leaves on some cross street that still boasted an anæmic tree or two. Saturday afternoons in Jersey—"Je's, it's a great day for football," he thought, idly, and swung into Sixty-seventh Street toward the Park.

Two elderly, gray-haired women twittered wren-like at the curb in front of a mountainous apartment house near Central Park West. They looked this way and that. At sight of Ernie's cab they fluttered their wings. He swooped down on them. They retreated timidly, then gave him the address and were swallowed in the maw of his taxi.

Two o'clock. Ernie's Saturday had begun.

The number they had given was on Lexington Avenue in the Fifties. It turned out to be a small motion-picture theater.

"This where you meant, lady?"

They fumbled with the door. Ernie reached in, opened it. They stepped out, stiffly. The fare was fifty-five cents. One wren handed him a minutely folded green bill. He tapped the change slot three times and gave her two dimes and a quarter. The wren put the three coins into a small black purse. From the same purse she extracted a five-cent piece and offered it to him. He regarded it impersonally, took it.

A little superstitious shiver shook him. A swell start for a Saturday, all right. What those two old birds want to come 'way over here to a bum movie for, anyway! Curious, he glanced at the picture title. *Souls for Sale.* That didn't sound so hot. Oh, well, you couldn't never tell what people done things for. He tucked the folded bill into his upper left coat pocket. He always did that with his first fare, for luck.

Off down the street. Might pick up a matinée fare one the hotels on Madison. He came down to Forty-seventh, jockeyed along the Ritz. Little groups of two and three stood on the steps and came languidly down to the sidewalk at the Madison Avenue entrance. Orchids, fur, sheer silk stockings, coonskin coats, yellow sticks: *au 'voir,* darling . . . *aw*fly nice. . . . The doorman hailed him.

Two of the orchids skipped into his car. They waved good-bye to a coonskin coat. Whyn't the big stiff come along with'm, pay their fare and maybe a decent tip instead of the dime these kind of janes give a guy?

"Listen, driver, can't you go faster?"

"Doing the best I can. You can't go ahead the lights."

Turn around the middle of the street front of the Amsterdam if the cop at Seventh wasn't looking. Yeh, he wasn't. "Forty-five cents."

"I've got it, dear. Please let me. Don't fuss. We're so late."

Oh, my Gawd!

The winning orchid handed him a dollar. He flipped a nickel and two quarters into his palm, turned to look hard. "That's all right," said the orchid. They skipped into the theater. Well, that was more like it. Cute couple kids, at that.

He headed down Eighth Avenue toward the loft district in the Thirties between Eighth and Fifth. The fur and cloak-and-suit manufacturers were rushed with late Saturday orders to be delivered, to be shipped. Little dark men ran up and down with swatches, with bundles, with packages of fur and cloth and felt. Take me down to Tenth and Fifth. Take me up to Thirty-second and Third. I want to go to Eighty-eight University Place.

It was tough driving through the packed greasy streets. You couldn't make time, but they were generous with their tips. Ernie preferred to stay all afternoon in and out of the cloak-and-suit district. Being too far downtown, he headed uptown again toward the Thirties. In Thirteenth Street, going west, vacant, he had a call from a gimlet-eyed young man at the curb in front of an old brick building. The young man leaned very close to Ernie. He made no move to enter the taxi. He glanced quickly up and down the street. He said to Ernie, quietly:

"Take a sack of potatoes?"

"Sure," said Ernie. "Where to?"

"Broadway and Nine'y-foist."

"Sure," said Ernie.

The gimlet-eyed young man nodded ever so slightly toward an unseen figure behind him. There emerged quickly from the doorway a short, mild-looking blond man. He carried a suitcase and a brown paper corded bundle. His strong short arms were tense-muscled under the weight of them. It was as though they held stone. He deposited these gently in the bottom of the cab. Glup-glup, came a soft gurgle. The younger man vanished as the little fellow climbed ponderously into the taxi. He reappeared carrying still another brown bundle. He sagged under it.

"Fi' bucks for you," he said to Ernie. "Take Ninth Avenue."

"Sure," said Ernie.

The young man closed the taxi door and disappeared into the brick building. Ernie and the mild blond fellow and the suitcase and the two stout, brown paper parcels sped up Ninth Avenue, keeping always on the far side of an occasional traffic cop and observing all road rules meticulously.

The uptown Broadway address reached, the man paid him his fare and the five dollars. Ernie sat stolidly in his seat while the little man wrestled with suitcase and bundles. Not him! They wouldn't catch Ernie carrying the stuff with his own hands. As the bundles touched the curb he stepped on the gas and was off, quickly. He headed down Broadway again.

A plump, agitated little woman in an expensive-looking black fur coat hailed him at Eighty-fifth. "Take me to Eight-fifty-five West End. And I'm late for a bridge game."

"That's terrible," said Ernie, grimly. She did not hear him. She perched on the edge of the seat, her stout silken legs crossed at the ankles, both feet beating a nervous tattoo.

Ernie whirled west on Eighty-fifth, then north up West End. The dressy woman climbed laboriously out. She handed Ernie his exact fare and scurried into the marble-and-plush foyer of Number Eight-fifty-five.

"And I hope you lose your shirt," Ernie remarked feelingly.

He took out the five-dollar bill that the man had given him for carrying the sack of potatoes, smoothed it and placed it in his billfold. Then he remembered the bill in his upper left coat packet—his first fare given him by the fluttery old ladies bent on seeing *Souls for Sale.* He fished down with two fingers, extracted the bill, smoothed it and said piously, "For the je's!"

It was a ten-dollar bill. His mind jolted back. He pieced the events of the past two hours into neat little blocks. Hm. Well. Gosh! Fifteen bones clean, he could

call it a day and knock off and go home and have dinner
with Jo. There was no possibility of returning the ten-
dollar bill to its owner, even if he had thought remotely
of so doing—which he emphatically had not.

The blue-and-gold doorman, guardian of Number
Eight-fifty-five, now approached Ernie. "What you
sticking around here blocking up this entrance?"

Ernie looked up absently. He tucked his bills tidily
into the folder, rammed the folder into his hip pocket.
"Do you want me to move on?" he inquired humbly.

"You heard me." But the doorman was suspicious
of such meekness.

Ernie shifted to first. He eyed the doorman tenderly.
"And just when I was beginning to love you," he
crooned.

Four-fifteen. He bumbled slowly around the corner on
Eighty-sixth and across to Columbus. Might go home,
at that. No, Jo wouldn't be there, anyway. A white-
tiled coffee shop. A great wire basket of golden-brown
doughnuts in the window, flaky-looking and flecked
with powdered sugar. Pretty cold by now. Ernie
stamped his feet. Guess he'd go in; have a cup of hot
coffee and a couple sinkers.

There were other hackmen in the steaming little
shop with its fragrance of coffee and its smell of sizzling
fat. They did not speak to Ernie nor he to them. The
beverage was hot and stimulating. He ate three crullers.

Feeling warm and gay, he climbed into the driver's seat again. He'd stick around a couple hours more. Then he'd go home and give the other guy a chance.

Down to Columbus Circle, across Fifty-ninth, down Seventh, across Fifty-seventh to Madison. Down Madison slowly. Not a call. Nearly five o'clock.

A girl gave him a call. Tall, slim, pale. Not New York. She had been standing at the curb. Ernie had seen her let vacant cabs go by. As she gave him the number she smiled a little. She looked him in the eye. Her accent was not New Yorkese. She got in. The number she had given turned out to be an office building near Fortieth.

"Wait here," she said and smiled again and looked into Ernie's eyes.

"Long?"

"No, just a minute. Please."

It didn't look so good. Still, he'd wait a couple minutes, anyway. Wonder was there another exit to this building.

She came out almost immediately. "The office was closed," she explained.

Ernie nodded. "Yeh, five o'clock, and Saturday afternoon. Close one o'clock."

She got into the taxi, gave another number. Ernie recognized it as being that of still another office building. That, too, probably would be closed, he told her.

He turned his head a little to look at her through the window.

She smiled and put her head on one side.

"I want to try, anyway." Then, as Ernie turned to face forward again, his hand on the gear shift, "Could I trouble you for a match?"

Hm. Thought so. When they asked you for a match, anything might happen. He gave her a light. She took it, lingeringly, and kept the matches. You want me to take you to that number, girlie? Yes. She did not resent the girlie. He took her to the number. Wait, please. In a minute she was back. Her voice was plaintive, her brow puckered.

"Seems like everybody's away," she said. She got in. "I love riding in taxis. I'm crazy about it." Her "I" was "Ah." Her *ou* was double *o*, or nearly.

"You from out of town?"

"I'm from Birmingham. I'm all alone in town. I guess you better take me to my hotel. The Magnolia Hotel, West Twenty-ninth."

He started for it, waiting for the next move from his fare. She pushed down the little seat that folded up, one of a neat pair, against the front of the taxi. She changed over to it and opened the sliding window, leaning out a little.

"My train doesn't go till ten o'clock tonight, and I haven't a thing to do till then."

"That's too bad," said Ernie.

"If I keep my room after six they charge for it. It's almost half-past five now. And my train doesn't go till ten and I haven't a thing to do."

"Yeh?"

"If I got my suitcase and checked out, would you be back down here at six?" They had reached the hotel entrance.

"Sure," said Ernie. She stepped out, her slim ankles teetering in high heels. She turned to go.

"Ninety cents, girlie," said Ernie. She gave him a dollar. Her hand touched his.

"Six o'clock," she repeated. "Right here."

"Sure," said Ernie.

He drove briskly over to the manufacturing section again. They were great taxi riders, those little dark paunchy men, and a fare there around six o'clock meant a good call up to the Bronx, or over to Brooklyn. The manufacturers worked late now in the height of the season. Six o'clock and often seven. On the way he got a call to Twelfth Street, came back to the Thirties, and there picked up a Bronx call just as he had hoped. This was his lucky day, all right. Breaking good. Wonder was that Birmingham baby standing on the curb, waiting.

He drove briskly and expertly in and out of the welter of traffic. His fare wanted some newspapers, and Ernie obligingly stopped at a newsstand and got them for him—*Sun, Journal, Mirror*. The man read them under the dim light inside the cab, smoking fat black cigars the while. The rich scent of them floated out to Ernie even through the tightly closed windows. A long cold ride, but Ernie didn't mind. He deposited his fare in front of a gaudy new apartment house far uptown.

"Cold night, my boy," said the man.

"I'll say!" A fifty-cent tip. The fare had left the newspapers in the taxi. Ernie selected the *Mirror*. He drove to a near-by lunchroom whose sign said Jack's Coffee Pot. Another cup of coffee and a ham-on-rye. He read his tabloid and studied its pictures, believing little of what he read. Sometimes, though rarely, he discussed notorious tabloid topics with a fellow worker, or with a talkative fare, or a lunchroom attendant. His tone was one of fly but judicious wisdom. In a murder trial he was not deceived by the antics of principals, witnesses, lawyers, or judges. "Yeh, well that baby better watch herself, because she can't get away with that with no jury. Blonde or no blonde, I bet she fries."

Seven-thirty. Guessed he'd start downtown and get around the Eighties by eight o'clock, pick up a nice theater fare. Wonder if that Birmingham baby was waiting yet. No. Too late. Looked as mild as skim-milk, too. Never can tell and that's a fact. He'd have to tell

Jo about that one—uh—no, guess he wouldn't, at that. Mightn't believe him. Women.

Central Park West. He turned in at Sixty-seventh, picked up a theater fare for Forty-fifth Street. Hoped that big bum on the corner Forty-fifth would leave him turn right, off Broadway. From Fifty-first to Forty-fifth his progress became a crawl, and the crawl became a series of dead stops punctuated by feeble and abortive attempts to move. The streets were packed solid. The sidewalks were a moving mass. Thousands of motors, tens of thousands of lights, hundreds of thousands of people.

Ernie sat unruffled, serene, watchful at his wheel. He rarely lost his temper, never became nervous, almost never cursed. It was too wearing. Hacking was no job for a nervous man. It was eight-thirty when he deposited his fare in front of the theater. Sometimes, on a good night, you could cover two theater calls. But this was not one of those nights. He went west to Ninth Avenue on his way to dinner uptown. Ninth would be fairly clear going. But at Forty-seventh and Ninth he reluctantly picked up a call headed for a nine-o'clock picture show. Oh, well, all right.

By nine he was again on his way uptown. He liked to eat dinner at Charley's place, the Amsterdam Lunch, on Amsterdam near Seventy-seventh. He could have stopped very well for a late dinner at home. But you never could tell. Besides, Jo getting a hot meal at nine— for what! The truth was that his palate had become accustomed to the tang of the pungent stews, the sharp sauces, and the hearty roughage of the lunchrooms and the sandwich wagons. When possible he liked to drive uptown to Charley's, out of the welter of traffic, where he could eat in nine-o'clock peace.

Charley was noted for his Blue Plate, 65c. He gave you stew or roast and always two fresh vegetables. Spinach and asparagus; corn and string beans. His peas were fresh. No canned stuff at Charley's. His potatoes were light and floury. Josie was an excellent cook. Yet, on the rare occasions when he ate at home, he consumed the meal listlessly, though dutifully. She went to endless trouble. She prepared delicate pastry dishes decorated with snarls of meringue or whipped cream. She cut potatoes into tortured shapes. She beat up sauces, stuffed fowl. Yet Ernie perversely preferred Smitty McGlaughlin's lunch wagon at Seventh and Perry.

Charley's long, narrow slit of a shop was well filled. There were only two empty stools along the glass-topped counter. Ernie had parked his car, one of a line of ten taxis, outside the Amsterdam Lunch.

"What's good eating tonight, Charley?" Ernie swung a leg over the stool at the counter.

Charley wore an artless toupee, a clean white apron,

a serious look. "Baked breast of lamb with peas and cauliflower and potatoes."

Ernie ordered it, and it was good. Rich brown gravy, and plenty of it. But even if, in Charley's momentary absence, you had made your own choice, you would not have gone wrong. Boiled ham knuckle, baked beans, Ger. fr., 50c. Broiled lamb chops, sliced tomatoes, Fr. fr., 55c. As you ate your Blue Plate there smirked up at you, through the transparent glass shelf below, sly dishes of apple pie, custards, puddings, cakes. Here you heard some of the gossip of the trade—tales of small adventure told in the patois of New York.

"I'm going East on Thirty-eighth, see, and the big harp standing there sees me, starts bawling me out, see? 'What the hell,' I says, 'what's eating into you?' Well, he comes up slow, see, stops traffic and walks over to me slow, looking at me, the big mick! 'Want a ticket, do you?' he says. 'Looking for it, are you?' he says. 'Asking for it? Well, take that,' he says, 'and like it.' Can you match that, the big . . ." There followed a stream of effortless obscenity almost beautiful in its quivering fluidity.

Usually, though, the teller emerged triumphant from these verbal or fistic encounters. "They give me a number up in Harlem. You ought to seen the pans of them. Scared you. When we get there it's in front of a light. So one of them pokes their head out of the window and says it ain't the place. It's in the next block, half-way. Well, then I know I'm right. I reached for the old jack handle under the seat and I climb down and open the door. 'Oh, yes it is,' I says. 'This is the right place, all right, and you're getting out.' At that the one guy starts to run. But the other swings back so I clip him one in the jaw. I bet he ain't come to yet—lookit the skin of my knuckles . . ."

His fellow diners listened skeptically and said he was an artist, thus conveying that he was a romancer of high imagination but low credibility. "Come on!" they said. "I heard you was hackin' at Mott Street Ferry all evening."

Ernie paid for his meal, took a toothpick, and was on his way downtown for the theater break. Might as well make a day of it. Get a good rest tomorrow. It was a grim business, this getting in line for the eleven-o'clock show crowd. The cops wouldn't let you stand, they wouldn't let you move. You circled round and round and round, east on Thirty-eighth, back to Broadway, chased off Broadway by the cops, east again, back up Broadway, over to Eighth. "Come on! Come on! *Come* ON!" bawled the cop, when you tried to get into Forty-second. "Come on! *Come* ON! COME ON!" chasing you up to Forty-fourth, on Eighth.

Ernie picked up a call in Forty-fourth. They wanted to go downtown to one of those Greenwich Village dumps. Pretty good call. Uptown again, and down again. He stopped at Smitty's and had a hamburger sandwich and a cup of coffee. Cold night, all right. How's hackin'? Good!

One o'clock. Might as well go over to the Sucker Clubs around the West Fifties. Saturday night you could pick up a $33\frac{1}{3}$. One of the boys had cleaned up a hundred dollars one night last week. You picked up a call that wanted to go to a night club—a club where there was enough to drink. You took him in, if he looked all right to you, and you handed him over to the proprietor and you parked your hack outside and you came in, comfortably, and waited—you waited with one eye on him and the other on the cash register. And no matter what he spent, you got your $33\frac{1}{3}$ percent. One, two, three hundred.

Ernie cruised about a bit, but with no luck. Half-past one. Guessed he'd call it a day and go home to old Jo and the hay. Early, though, for a Saturday night. Pretty fair day.

He cruised across Fifty-first Street, slowly, looking carefully up at the grim old shuttered houses, so quiet, so quiet. A door opened. A bar of yellow light made a gash in the blackness. Ernie drew up at the curb. A man appeared at the top of the stairs. He was supporting a limp bundle that resembled another man. The bundle had legs that twisted like a scarecrow's.

"Hello, Al," said Ernie.

"Hey," called the man, softly, "give me a hand, will you?"

Ernie ran up the stairs, took the scarecrow under the left arm as the man had it under the right arm. The bundle said, with dignity: "Cut the rough stuff, wil! you, you big bum?"

Ernie, surprised, looked inquiringly at Al. "His head is all right," Al explained. "He ain't got no legs, that's all."

Together they deposited the bundle in Ernie's hack. Ernie looked at the face. It was scarred again and again. There were scars all over it. Old scars. It was Benny Opfer.

"There!" said Al, affably, arranging the legs and stepping back to survey his handiwork. "Now, then. The address——"

"I'll give my own address," interrupted Mr. Opfer, with great distinctness, "you great big so-and-so."

Al withdrew. The yellow gash of light showed again briefly; vanished. The house was dark, quiet.

Benny Opfer gave his address. It was in Brooklyn.

"Oh, say," protested Ernie, with excusable reluctance, "I can't take no call to Brooklyn this time of night."

"Do you know who I am?" Ernie was no weakling;

but that voice was a chill and horrid thing, coming even as it did from the limp and helpless body.

"Yeh, but listen, Mr. Opfer——"

"Brooklyn." He leaned forward ever so little by an almost superhuman effort of will. "I'm a rich man. When I was fourteen I was earning a hundred dollars a week."

"That right!" responded Ernie wretchedly.

"Do you know how?"

"Can't say I do."

"Gunning," said Mr. Benny Opfer modestly. And sank back.

They went to Brooklyn.

Arrived at the far Brooklyn destination, "I ain't got any money," announced Mr. Benny Opfer with engaging candor, as Ernie lifted him out.

"Aw, say, listen," objected Ernie plaintively. He hoisted Mr. Benny Opfer up the steps and supported him as he fitted the key.

"Get you some," Opfer promised him. "She's always got fi' dollars stuck away some place. You wait."

"I'll wait inside," Ernie declared stoutly.

Ernie stood outside in the cold November morning. He looked up at a lighted upper window of the Brooklyn house. Sounds floated down, high shrill sounds. He waited. He mounted the steps again and rang the bell, three long hard rings. He came down to the street again and looked up at the window. 'Way over to Brooklyn, and then gypped out of his fare! He rang the bell again and again.

The window sash was lifted. A woman's head appeared silhouetted against the light behind it. "Here!" she called softly. Something dropped at Ernie's feet. It was the exact fare. Benny Opfer, limp as to legs, had been level-headed enough when it came to reading the meter.

Half-past three.

Ernie was on his way home, coming up Third Avenue at a brisk clip. A man and girl hailed him. The girl was pretty and crying. The man gave an address that was Riverside at 118th Street. The streets were quiet now. Quiet. Sometimes New York was like that for one hour, between three-thirty and four-thirty. The front window was open an inch or two.

"You don't need him," said the man. "He's all washed up. You stick to me and everything'll be all right. He never was on the level with you, anyway."

"I'm crazy for him," whimpered the girl.

"You'll be crazy about me in a week. I'm telling you."

An early morning L train roared down her reply.

Cold. Getting colder all the time. Sitting here since one o'clock today. Today! Yesterday. Ernie sank his neck into his sweater and settled down for the grind up to 118th. Last fare he'd take, not if it was the governor of New York state, he wouldn't.

The man and the girl got out. The girl's head drooped on the man's shoulder. The man paid Ernie. She wouldn't sit so pretty with that bimbo if the size of his tip was any sign and, if it wasn't, what was?

No more hackin' this night. He turned swiftly into Broadway.

Tired. Dead tired. Kind of dreamy, too. This hackin'. Enough to make you sick to your stomach. Taking everybody home and putting them to bed. Just a goddam wet-nurse, that's what. One Hundred and Fifteenth. Tenth. His eye caught a little line of ice that formed a trail down the middle of Broadway. The milk wagons that came down from the station at 125th Street. The melting ice inside these trickled through the pipe to the pavement, making a thin line of ice in the cold November morning. One Hundredth. Ninety-fifth.

Half-past four.

The sound of a tremendous explosion. The crash of broken glass. Ernie, relaxed at the wheel, stiffened into wakeful attention. It was still dark. He drove swiftly down to Ninetieth Street. The remains of a white-painted milk wagon lay scattered near the curb. Broken glass was everywhere. A horse lay tangled in the reins. The sound of groans, low and unceasing, came from within the shattered wagon. Fifty feet away was a powerful car standing upright and trim on the sidewalk.

Ernie drew up, got out. All about, in the towering apartment houses lining the street, windows were flung open. Heads stuck out. Police whistles sounded. No policeman appeared. Ernie went over to the cart; peered in. A man lay there, covered with milk and blood and glass. Chunks of glass stuck in his cheeks, in his legs. They were embedded in his arms. He was bleeding terribly and groaning faintly as he bled. More faintly. Men appeared—funny fat men and lean men in pajamas with overcoats thrown on.

"Here, give me a hand with this guy," commanded Ernie. "He's bleeding to death."

No one came forward. Blood. They did not want to touch it. Ernie looked up and around. He saw a figure emerge from the queerly parked automobile and walk away, weaving crazily.

"Hey, get that bird," cried Ernie, "before he gets away. He's the one hit this wagon. Must of been going eighty miles an hour, the way this outfit looks."

A slim, pale young fellow, fully dressed, detached himself from the crowd that had now gathered—still no police—walked quickly across the street—seemed almost to flow across it, like a lean cat. He came up behind the man who had emerged from the reckless automobile. Swiftly he reached into his back hip pocket, took from it a blackjack, raised his arm lightly, brought it down on the man's head. The man crumpled slowly to the pavement. The pale young fellow vanished.

The groans within the shattered wagon were much fainter. "Give me a hand here," commanded Ernie again. "One you guys. What's eating you! Scared you'll get your hands dirty! Must of all been in the war, you guys."

Someone helped him bundle the ludicrous yet terrible figure into the taxi. Ernie knew the nearest hospital, not five minutes away. He drove there, carefully yet swiftly. The groans had ceased. Men in white uniforms received the ghastly burden.

Ernie looked ruefully at the inside of his hack. Pools of red lay on the floor, on the cushions; ran, a viscid stream, down the steps.

At the garage, "I won't clean no car like that," declared the washer.

"All right, sweetness, all right," snarled Ernie. "I'll clean it tomorrow myself."

The washer peered in, his eyes wide. "Je's, where'd you bury him!" he said.

Josie was asleep, but she awoke at his entrance, as she almost always did.

"How'd you make out, Ernie?"

"Pretty good," replied Ernie, yawning. "Made a lot of jack."

"You rest till late," Josie murmured drowsily. "Then

in the afternoon we'll maybe go to a movie or some-wheres. There's *Ride 'em, Cowboy* at the Rivoli."

"The West," said Ernie, dreamily, as he took off his socks. "That's the place where I'd like to go. 'Ride 'em, Cowboy!' That's the life. Nothing ever happens in this town."

WALL STREET -'28

Leetle Lettie

EDNA FERBER

WALL STREET—'28

1928

Edna Ferber

WALL STREET—'28

THOUGH he breakfasted each morning at eight-thirty, Cass Condon always breakfasted in twilight. Eighteen thousand a year, though a goodly rental, does not insure perfection in a New York apartment. When the Condons had taken the place, nine years ago, even the dining room had been bright. Flooded—as the agent had daringly put it—with sunshine. How could they have known, even in this maniacal city, that the substantial twelve-story building on the south was almost immediately to be tumbled down and whisked away like a child's house of blocks, and a twenty-story apartment house shot up in its place, plunging the Condon dining room into gloom?

For that matter, Hilda Condon argued, suppose you did move to one of those roof apartments among the clouds! You might very well wake up some morning to find that a modern Aladdin had caused newer and higher roofs to spring up about you overnight, hemming you in so that you on your roof were really living at the bottom of a well.

155

Then, too, moving was such a hideous process. All of Cass's books; new carpets (they never could be made to fit); and running around Madison Avenue matching things and quarreling with decorators. Besides, this was as nearly perfect as most apartments of its class. It was something of a landmark (ten years old); the rooms were large and lofty, on the fourteenth floor, at Park Avenue and Fifty-fourth Street.

Though the dining room was dim, all the others were bright enough—except, of course, the kitchen and the maids' quarters. The drawing room, a gracious thirty-five-foot expanse, boasted six windows commanding an uninterrupted view of the windows of the apartment house on the opposite corner of Park Avenue and Fifty-fourth Street.

Hilda Condon had solved the problem of the dim dining room by causing gold gauze curtains to be hung. They gave the effect of synthetic sunlight as Cass drank his morning orange juice.

That orange juice never had so much as a seedlet afloat on its surface. Certainly Hilda Condon could pride herself on the gift of making a man comfortable. A perfectly managed household. Fresh bed linen daily. Cass's soap dish never was gelatinous. Hilda never said who was that on the phone, dear. There was his room; there was her room; a dressing room between.

Hilda had done his room as carefully as hers. Very

male it was, with dark solid furniture vaguely Italian, many books, and a jumble of Wall Street and highbrow magazines; on the wall a Van Gogh nude posterior view of a sturdy woman, slightly knock-kneed. Cass had bought that. Hilda thought it hideous.

In the perfumed and orderly dressing room were shelved closets holding piles of great soft bath towels, embroidered hand towels, gay washcloths, and rosy stacks of Hilda's exquisite undergarments over which women in the provinces of France had bent their gaze to pick out gossamer threads in order to put in their place other gossamer threads in a pattern of embroidery and hemstitching.

Then Hilda's room, with its chaise-longue, its silk-petticoated dressing table, the scent of expensive perfume, and a battalion of jars and flasks flashing orange and amber and jade in the rosy lamplight.

When the curtains of the apartment were all drawn (you pulled a slender cord and they advanced on each other, two by two, like figures in a quadrille) the place shut you in with its warmth, its secrecy, its intimacy.

Cass was a Wall Street broker by trade and terribly rich in a quiet way. Cass Condon and old Cass before him had always had so much money that they had learned the discomfort and futility of spending a lot in the hope of making oneself completely comfortable. They had one motorcar, Hilda's, and Cass practically never rode in that. Hilda never could understand his horror of owning Things—country houses, motors, opera boxes—fat plush Things.

He fraternized with men who owned these Things in numbers. It irked Hilda terribly that he, too, would not summon the rich beautiful objects at his command. He actually preferred to ride in taxis, for example. She had been Hilda Whatsis of the Long Island Whatsises. A comfortable woman to live with. They had been married thirteen years. . . . Can't I drop you somewhere, dear? I'm putting you next to that pretty Passavant girl at dinner, and I guess that makes me a pearl among wives. . . . Why don't you snatch forty winks before time to dress? . . . She knew the colors he preferred; the foods that agreed with him; his taste in clothes, women, music, books. In their talks she often could have told you what he was going to say before he said it.

She knew nothing about him.

"Me, I'm married," she sometimes admitted, gayly, to her intimates, "to that gent you read about—the Tired Business Man. Of course I know it's horrible Down There. From nine to five he's under terrific strain. So I try to see to it that he's relaxed and amused and stimulated after hours. If it weren't for me he'd grub like a mole between this house and his office. If I didn't make him see and do beautiful things once in a while—— Why, poor darling, I've actually known him to fall asleep at the opera, like the fellow in the funny papers. One night—I remember it was the Russian Ballet—Prince Igor—you know, all that gorgeous color and movement—I nudged him, and he opened his eyes and looked sort of glassily at the stage a moment and said, very solemnly, 'Pooh!' and shut them again. When we got home I asked him what he had meant, but he only answered, 'If I said pooh I must have meant pooh.'"

They were always the same, the routine rites performed by Cass preliminary to issuing forth at nine. A shower, hot and cold; an abstemious breakfast, with a lightning first-page glance; a look in to see if Hilda was awake amidst her pillows and her ostrich and her pink. Hilda was one of those women who appear very well in bed, though perhaps a shade ocherous at nine A. M. She was marshaling her day.

". . . really wish you'd speak to Otto, because yesterday the car looked filthy . . . seven sharp because we're dining early with the Gebhardts before the theater . . . your coat, even if the sun is shining, because Nettie says it's quite nippy . . . remember to see about the tickets for the nineteenth . . . cut yourself . . . why a man with millions chooses to shave himself! . . ."

He kissed her.

Cass Condon always walked from his apartment at Fifty-fourth down Park Avenue to Thirty-fourth. One

New York mile. On the way he saw other men like himself walking a self-conscious mile toward Wall Street, clothed in expensive well-tailored garments, treading the pavement in hand-made shoes, their gait, oh, so springy. At Thirty-fourth he hailed a taxi.

Sometimes, on a brilliant spring day, if he happened to be a bit early, he would alight a block or two short of his office building and walk the rest of the way for the sheer exhilaration the sight afforded him.

He thought—not very originally—that the street was like a chasm in a mountain range, the Woolworth Tower one of its loftiest peaks. Those white shafts were so dazzling against the crashing blue of the sky. He wondered if, some day, those shafts would seem huts compared to others that would soar in their place. Or would the whole Island, perhaps, yielding to the pressure put upon its base, crumple under the weight of the latest gigantic monolith, and tipping inch by inch, slip slowly into the Bay of New York?

He pictured the frantic crowds rolling pell-mell down the narrow streets, over and over, clutching futilely at the spire of Trinity, grabbing at the tip of the Woolworth Building, clinging to a fiftieth-floor parapet as they whirled and bounded by, only to end inevitably as wriggling specks in the sunken island of débris made up of granite and brick and steel and men and women; the topmost stone of the highest skyscraper and the nethermost slab of the oldest gravestone in Trinity churchyard all mingling and blending in affable accord at last. Time and progress in the discard where they belonged.

. . . tickets for the nineteenth . . . speak to Otto . . . seven sharp . . .

Half-past nine. This was the malest street in the world. They poured into it—into this region known as Wall Street—from the "L" trains and the subways, from ferries and surface lines and taxis—men and men and men, all curiously young and all curiously alike in some indefinable way.

The Street had a vitality so terrific that it struck you with the impact of a blow. No other street in the world was so alive, so overwhelming. There were women here, too, but they were in the minority. Cass liked to see them coming briskly to work, so fantastically out of place in this world of finance.

They appeared very businesslike and efficient and absurd in their smart slim dresses and their silk stockings and their little high-heeled shoes. Sometimes you saw one of them looking down at the pavement as she went, her head cocked a little to one side, like a bird; or you saw her looking up at the sky and bumping into other pedestrians, and as she walked thus her lips were wreathed in loveliness, and she smiled a little secret smile.

The *whish-whoosh* of the revolving doors that led into

his granite mountain was as steady and relentless as the surge of the sea against a cliff.

He stepped into one of the thirty bronze elevators. Cass's father, old Cass, in his day had been able to exchange a morning greeting with the grizzled veteran who manned the convulsive lift in the old building that had then housed the solid firm of Minch & Condon: Good-morning, Pete! Good-morning, Mr. Condon, good-morning! And how are you this fine April day? None of that between Cass and this tight white gimlet-eyed young Icarus who slammed the great bronze gates in an Olympian clangor of great bronze gates being slammed all about him. That sort of pleasantry had no place in this grimmer, sterner day. Millionaire brokers were no treat to the employee of a building that housed a hundred of them.

"Three out!" called a passenger. Three out meant that someone wished to stop at the thirtieth floor.

"Four out!" The lift swooped to the fortieth.

Cass's office was not so high, but high enough. Through the outer office where clerks already were tick-tacking with chalk on blackboards; down the corridor; into his own office. It was not the room itself, though that was well enough. Fawn color, beige, and blue. A vast walnut desk over which time and an artist in the cabinetmaker's ancient craft had spread a deep delectable patina like hot maple fudge. But it was past all this that the eye leaped to the windows.

The world lay spread below Cass Condon's office windows. They were huge windows, high, wide, and thick to withstand the western gales. Cass Condon actually spent half his day looking out of his office windows. He himself did not realize this. He was like one hypnotized by the shifting beauty of what lay there. He probably would have denied that he drifted to those windows twenty times a day and stood there twenty minutes at a time. But it was true.

There he stood, Cass Condon, stockbroker, in his stockbroking office a quarter of a mile up in the air; and all about him was high piercing beauty like the music Kreisler makes on his violin. A fifty-story building pointed toward the sky like a white finger taunting God. Looking down, you saw the scarlet and black and orange funnels of mammoth ocean liners resting in their slips, and they were toys that little boys pull by a string in the park pond. The dockyards were etchings of black and gray and smoky white. To the south, toward Rector Street, lived the Armenian and Syrian families huddled in the decayed splendor of the old mansions where once had dwelt the prosperous Dutch and English of another day—shipping men, merchants, solid families. Now central and eastern Europe hung its exhilarating washing on lines between the areaways, where it whirled and flaunted a frieze of blue and orange and scarlet and purple and pink against the dingy courtyards below. Beyond this lay Battery Park, sunning itself. From that the eye traveled the breadth of the North River with what not of craft darting like gadflies on its surface.

Cass had stood at his window above the river while a President had gone majestically by on his way to Europe a hero and had returned a broken old man. Troop ships had gone by, and ships bearing queens and generals and aviators; bands playing, flags flying, hats in the air. Beyond this lay the Bay of New York, Ellis Island, the Kill Van Kull, the open ocean. And just there, on the opposite shore of the river, Jersey, and back, back to where the blue-gray outlines of the Orange hills were dimly sketched against the sky.

A sight, surely, to have blanched the visage of one of the sturdy red-faced Dutch settlers of three hundred years ago; a sight shocking in its force and vigor and exhilaration.

There it lay for Cass Condon to see. It moved and changed and shifted daily, hourly, momentarily. It was thus at ten, and thus-and-so at noonday, and quite another thing in color and form in the early winter twilight. He felt exhilarated and powerful and free in his office. Nowhere else. He did not know this.

Prince Igor indeed!

Miss Rosen. Miss Rosen knocked and entered. She bore his mail, all neatly documented, and the papers over which his expert eye would travel, digesting the cryptic figures at a glance. Anaconda, Mont., said the letters; Del Monte, Cal.; New Orleans, Denver, Waco, Yazoo City, Little Rock, Chattanooga, San Francisco, Macon.

"Hello, Miss Rosen! Good-morning." He turned from the window. "Anything to get excited about?"

"Good-morning. Uh no. The usual stuff."

Miss Rosen was a tall, well-built big girl with abundant reddish hair worn long and parted in the middle. In coloring and conformation she was like the women you see in the old Italian paintings, and had an effect very restful amidst the beige and blue and fawn of Cass's office. Her clothes were in excellent taste, smart, becoming, expensive. She was efficient, but feminine. Miss Rosen never had married. She got (and earned) ten thousand a year which an occasional lucky flier swelled to fifteen.

She could, if necessary, have run the firm of Minch & Condon single-handed. She had worked downtown since she was sixteen. There was nothing she did not know about Cass Condon's business. No letter reached him that she had not first scanned. No letter reached him that was not worth his scanning. His telephone calls passed first through her. She separated the gold from the dross, the goats from the lambs; she was the alimentary tract which predigested Cass Condon's tasks for him.

The men she met in the course of her business day in Wall Street had spoiled her taste for the kind of men she might meet in her ordinary social contacts. Her family said she was stuck up, and so she was. Miss Rosen's family squatted on her broad shoulders; sat hunched there; possessed her, fed on her. It was her unrealized dream to live in a two-room apartment in the East Fifties, alone. Sometimes she went to the theater, to a concert. Her escape came when she left the house at quarter-past eight in the morning.

The relation between Cass and Miss Rosen was friendly, cozy, intimate and innocent. Miss Rosen was not in the least in love with him, nor he with her. Miss Rosen understood him better than his wife. She knew more about him than did any other human being in the world. She liked him. She reminded him of wedding anniversaries, birthdays, insurance premiums, taxes, tailor's appointments. Her taste was exquisite and unerring. She could select an emerald or a box of candy.

"Do you like this tie, Miss Rosen?"

She would turn upon it the appraising gaze of her warm brown eyes with the little gold flecks in them.

"Not much. I think it's a little sissy—all that blue. Mrs. Condon selected it, didn't she?"

"How did you know?"

"Well, women think men's ties should match their eyes. You look better in more masterful colors."

Hilda disliked her. They were very polite to each other.

By this time Cass knew the trend of the day's market, had digested his mail, had read the trade sheets, had manipulated his own business through such speedy media as the cable, telegraph, telephone, and Miss Rosen. Through and above and about all this, like a motif in a symphony, he swung back to the window and he wandered over to the ticker. He never tired of the Esperanto of the ticker tape as it spewed up its story, chittering fortune or disaster.

UNC $50\frac{7}{8}$ STU $62\frac{3}{4}$ WEP. VIR VKK GHR 27
EPU $2.41\frac{7}{8}$ TX $10.52\frac{1}{2}$ WA

It reminded him vaguely of something. Of the talk at one of Hilda's dinners: Seven sharp because we're something or other early with the Gebhardts . . . third hand high . . . they say she won't give him a divorce and can you blame her after all . . . I go down there for the sunshine. I don't care for all that gambling and society God knows I get enough of that right here but you take the Bath and Tennis Club beach for example at noon why there's nothing on the Riviera can touch it . . . little Paris model but modified of course they can't put in a tailored sleeve decently but when it comes to evening clothes you have to hand it . . . did you hear the one about the drunk in the subway it seems he . . .

A directors' meeting at eleven.

That long bare mahogany table; those long bare mahogany faces, burned red brown from golf at Aiken, at Palm Beach, and Pinehurst.

They were not solemn as their fathers had been before them, gathered at similar mahogany oblongs under like circumstances. They did not smoke fat black cigars. Their stomachs were concave, their faces rather expressionless. Like the men in the street below they all strangely resembled one another. It was not an actual similarity of features. It was as though, after being finished, each had been coated with a glaze of varnish out of the same pot.

There were nine of them at this meeting. Their attitude toward each other was affable, easy, slightly humorous. An outsider would have been puzzled to know why these men had met so formally at this hour of the morning. They talked of golf scores, of the races at Belmont, of transatlantic flying and the respective merits of this car and that. They conversed quietly, and laughed a little, but not too jovially. When they turned to the actual business in hand they disposed of it quickly and tersely, tossing millions lightly into the air. Cigarettes at fifteen cents a pack came out of gold and platinum cases from Cartier's. Capital stock seventy million. Surplus million million. Resources billion billion billion. They talked smoothly and composedly.

The room was quiet, quiet, high up above the city. Through the broad windows you saw little April puffball clouds chasing each other like kittens across the blue sky.

Well, gentlemen, I think that concludes our business.

Scarcely half an hour had gone by. A soft-stepping girl went round the table giving to each of the nine two bright new-minted twenty-dollar gold pieces and one ten-dollar gold piece. In old Cass's day a director's fee had been one ten or one twenty. Cass always gave his directors'-meeting gold pieces to Hilda.

There was now a little more of the amiable desultory talk as they broke up. Summer plans. Stocks. The market in the last two weeks had gone mad. A new buying record had been established. Thousands of little people ran around buying thousands of little things named Gen Mo and Int Har and Am Rad and Gen Elec. The scene on the Stock Exchange, always pandemonium, had reached a height of frenzy beyond description. Judgment Day would see no sight more chaotic.

On his way back to his office Cass Condon dropped by to look at this as Nero looked on while Rome burned. Thousands of tiny black ants ran to and fro making a crazy pattern of movement, and out of this pattern Cass actually could decipher a meaning. He could even, in

that welter, pick the particular ants whose scurryings
had to do with the firm of Minch & Condon. Out of
these scurryings had come to Cass sums with which
Hilda could have rented fifty apartments at the corner
of Park Avenue and Fifty-fourth Street; could have
bought fifty motorcars; given fifty thousand dinners
for the Gebhardts.

Back to the window and the ticker. The ticker was
gibbering more idiotically than ever. The window revealed the brilliance of an April noonday with a high
mad wind. Bits of paper sailed up half a mile in the air
and pretended they were gulls, swooping and dipping
and whirling.

"I'm going out to lunch, Miss Rosen. Tell Soandso
thisandthat. I'll be back at two."

Trinity churchyard was full of loungers basking in
the spring. Clerks sprawled like lean lizards in the sun.
Little stenographers perched on the flat slabs of ancient
gravestones and munched apples and read Sabatini.

Liberty Street at noonday was a gray and black
chiaroscuro. Nassau Street opened out brilliant and
startling. The sunlight was like a sword thrust. You felt
as if you had been plunged into cold water and then hot.

Cass lunched at his club, a cozy nook on the forty-
eighth floor of the Bond Building. The room was vaulted
and tiled. The food was well cooked and perfectly
served. The windows to the south side framed the bay;

to the north lay the city, a vast Persian carpet of color for gods like Cass to tread upon.

He ate a cautious and deliciously prepared luncheon, being full-blooded and not very healthy, with a tendency toward gout inherited from old Cass and fostered by a good deal of indiscreet eating and drinking in his youth. The oyster bar at the far end tempted him. He had a bowl of stew, eschewing the bivalves; crackers, celery and a baked apple. He lunched usually with the same group of men at the same table. The talk was interesting and even amusing. Sometimes they had a guest—the newest aviator or French diplomat or Russian tenor. No woman was ever allowed in the room. In these safe precincts one could have wine, cocktails, beer, ale. Almost no one availed himself of this privilege.

When Cass returned to his office Miss Rosen was there with more papers, more letters, things written on slips. Everything in order. She was composed but vivacious. A stimulating but restful person, Miss Rosen.

"Isn't it grand out! I don't see why people want to go to the country in April when it's so much more like spring down here. I skipped in a minute to see the Easter altar decorations at Trinity. The lilies were lovely."

"You'll have to eat an extra matzoth tonight in penance."

"There's a long strip of ticker tape that the wind

picked up and twisted round the church spire. Look.
You can see it from here. There! Like a pennant. I don't
know. I came out feeling kind of married."

Cass, understanding, grinned.

From the window he turned to the ticker again as a
mother lays a finger on the forehead and pulse of a
feverish child.

From the telephone on his desk came a single ring.
Mr. Heavenrich on the phone.

Mr. Wally Heavenrich was president of Behemoth
Pictures, Inc. Cass had a great block of Behemoth
Pictures, Inc., which he used for amusement rather than
profit. He almost never saw a picture, but he was repaid
by the immense entertainment provided by a first-hand
study of the mind and manners of Mr. Wally Heavenrich.

"Hello, Cass! How are you, Cass? Listen, Cass, I want
you to come over here to my office at four, won't you,
Cass, and take a look at a picture we're running
through."

"I'm due at the gym at half-past three. Anyway, you
know I don't look at pictures."

"But listen, Cass, this is different. I wish you would
do me a favor and come up and see this picture. Listen,
Cass. This is a picture if the German producers think
they have all the artistic pictures let me tell you they
are going to get fooled this time. The Coast just sent it

on and the girl in it is going to be the sensation of Broadway, mark my words. They're tired of these Swedish
masseuses and Polish Hunkies and this couch stuff.
This little girl is the first real ingénue since Pickford.
She reminds you of your first sweetheart when you
went to school. I'll send the car for you at the gym.
What do you want more than half an hour of that bag-
punching or whatever it is, a big strapping boy like you!
I have got some Scotch Leon brought me from England
it is like a liqueur."

"I never touch the stuff."

"All right, Cass, all right. Come anyway. A favor
to me, Cass."

At three Cass left the window and the ticker tape
and Miss Rosen and the Street behind him. At three-
fifteen he was doing a lot of undignified things that
resembled the antics of an overturned beetle. He lay on
his back and alternately brought his right and left leg
up in the air and down slowly within two inches of the
floor; he did half-somersaults; he turned over on his
face and chinned the ground, his biceps screaming. He
then put on gloves and tried to jab the jaw of a mosquito
made of steel springs and named McDermott. The
mosquito treated him disrespectfully, saying, "Yeah,
you couldn't hit a barn door with a shovel." Queerly
enough Cass did not seem to resent this. Hot, wet, and
red-faced, he then stood under an ice-cold shower.

At four he entered a Madison Avenue building which was the fruit of what happens when an American architect travels in Spain. He was ushered through halls and corridors by troops of attendants and glorified office boys and terrifically dressy secretaries and came at last to the cathedral spaces of Wally Heavenrich's private office where he sank in plush and hand-tooled leather to his chin. He refused the Scotch and the cigar out of the ancient and beautiful box which had been part of the jewel treasure of an Italian church and was now so cleverly converted into a humidor.

"This girl, I am telling you, Cass, is a type which———"

"All right, all right. You're a throwback to the slave market in Damascus."

Curiously enough, Wally Heavenrich was right. Cass Condon, looking at the picture, would not have believed that anyone could be so right as he had been about this girl. Her name was Emmy Dale and she hailed from Iowa, and she was the most exquisite and touching little figure he had ever seen. After the lean voluptuous ladies of the screen, stretched pantherlike on impermanent-looking couches, she seemed from another world.

Her arms had the immature curves of adolescence. Her profile still was haunted by the piquant spirit of childhood. Her mouth was soft and wet and flexible, like a puppy's, and her eyes said, "I trust you." Looking at her you resolved to be kinder to your office staff, more generous with your wife, more tolerant of your friends; to give up desserts, do something about that widening bald spot, buy some new shirts. Youth. That was it. She made you young again.

The picture was terrible, and she triumphed above it. Wally Heavenrich sat beside Cass and kept up a maddening buzz of comment. Cass Condon ignored it. Here was sheer loveliness of body and mind and spirit in a world where he had thought it had ceased to exist.

The picture ran its foolish length, and there was nothing that Emmy Dale did that was not perfect.

Cass Condon frequently day-dreamed of the perfect woman. When he read or heard of the futile excesses of men like himself—forty-fivish, rich, respected—he did not condemn them. He understood something of their unsatisfied longing. In a perverted way they were little boys looking for the rainbow's end. . . . Stanford White . . . What's-his-name . . . that girl they found murdered . . . Hilda was a good kid, amusing, balanced, poised, but . . .

"If you'd care to meet her," Wally was saying, "she's over at the Ambassador with her mother. She never goes anywhere without her mother. She doesn't go around like these others. Half the time she's got a book under her arm. She is a student, that kid is."

Cass was for walking. The Ambassador was a scant half-dozen blocks away.

"Oh, no!" cried Wally Heavenrich, in shocked accents. "My car is right here. . . . Fred, take us over to the Ambassador. Over to the Ambassador, Fred."

"Yes, Mr. Heavenrich. The Ambassador?"

"Yes, Fred, the Ambassador."

"If you say that again I'll bust you," said Cass suddenly, his face red.

"Say what?" Mr. Heavenrich smiled as one who does not quite understand the joke, but is willing to.

"That. The Ambassador."

"Ambassador!"

"Oh, my God!"

Mr. Heavenrich in the Ambassador was greeted like royalty. How do you do, Mr. Heavenrich. Good-evening, Mr. Heavenrich. How are you this evening, Mr. Heavenrich? His was a triumphal progress from car to door, from door to elevator, from elevator to the portal of Miss Dale's apartment. Mr. Heavenrich was no slouch himself when it came to greetings. He, too, knew names. The doorman, the hall boys, the elevator man. Hello, Louis. H'are yuh, Ed? Evening, Sid. Fine, George. How are *you?*

"We'll surprise her. We'll go right up. She'll be home, that little bookworm . . ." The noise within Miss Dale's apartment was such as to render their knock or buzz unavailing, so they entered.

The little bookworm was standing in the center of the

splendid room in a little black velvet dress and a little Fauntleroy lace collar and little low-heeled pumps. Cass Condon knew it was she by the way she resembled the girl he had just seen in the picture. Someone was playing the piano, very loud. Wally Heavenrich and Cass Condon stood in the doorway. As she turned and saw them she suddenly and miraculously not only resembled the girl of the picture; she became that girl. The thing slipped down over her face like a smooth fluid mask. She was even a better actress than Cass had thought.

She came straight over to them. She ran to them, like a child. "Oh, Mr. Heavenrich, why didn't you let me know! You bad man, you!"

"Hello, girlie! Do you know who this is I've got with me! This is Mr. Cass Condon, and you better be nice to him."

"Nice! I'm thrilled! I'm really scared to death. As if I didn't know who Mr. Cass Condon was! Everybody knows who Mr. Cass Condon is, I guess."

She stood before him, looking up at him. Somewhere inside her must be the fine white flame that had burned through the girl of the picture. There was something infinitely touching about her meager little shoulders, her too-slim legs. He looked down at her, feeling almost sheepish, like a boy. Hoping he did not look it. Absurd. She was talking.

"Won't you have a cocktail? Well, I never touch them, either. But you have to have them for other people or they won't come. Won't you have even a teensy one? You don't need to be afraid of my gin, because it's good old Piccadil—uh—dear old Wally told me it was pre-war Piccadilly, whatever that means. . . ."

Something inside Cass Condon was sinking.

"I'm afraid I must be running along, Miss Dale. I just dropped in——"

Her little hand clutched his arm. Wally Heavenrich was talking to a girl at the far end of the room.

"Oh, Mr. Condon, don't go. I want to talk to you. I want you to advise me." She looked up at him with the limpid eyes of the girl in the picture.

"Glad to. But what could I advise you about that Heavenrich, for example, wouldn't know a lot better?"

"Oh, but he doesn't! He wouldn't. Come over here and sit down." The fellow at the piano was playing furious discords. Cass had a curious feeling that he was playing at him. "Now tell me, honestly, what did you think of me in the picture?"

He told her.

She looked a little bewildered. The terms he used were not in her vocabulary, but she sensed that they were meant in praise and admiration. Then her lovely mouth puckered into a pout. "But that's just it. They want me to keep on playing those parts because I look it.

They won't let me play any other kinds. But I want to play something where I can wear clothes—beautiful clothes—and look like something. In a picture like the one you saw this afternoon I am just playing myself and I don't think that is acting. I don't think that is true Art. Anyway a girl has got to look out for her future, and look at what happened to Mary. She played those little innocent parts all the time and pretty soon she got too old for them—of course I'm so young—I mean I guess I don't have to start worrying for a long time yet, but anyway I am like that. I think of my future and look ahead of my career. And you can't play parts like that when you're an old hag of twenty-five."

"I think you were exquisite in it," Cass said again, helplessly. He had to get out. What was the matter with that fellow at the piano? He was staring at him with an almost hypnotic fixity of gaze; playing at him in a kind of frenzy. "Who's that fellow? What's he rolling his eyes at me for?"

"That! Oh, Mr. Condon, I want you to meet him. You must. Isn't he wonderful?"

"I'm afraid I must be running along, Miss Dale."

"That's one of his own things he's playing. I think he's a million times better than Gershwin only people have got so used to saying Gershwin Gershwin all the time. I don't see where Gershwin's so hot. He's dying to meet you. Won't you come over and meet him? Oh, my!

I keep forgetting you're a great man. Let me bring him over to you, I mean. Listen. He has written an opera and all he needs is somebody who understands and appreciates good music to help him produce it. I want you to let him play a little of——"

"Some other time. Glad to. Charmed. I've just got to go . . . Hey, Wally. I'm going. Late already. My wife—promised my wife I'd be home . . ."

Wally seemed relieved, if anything. He had been regarding them from the other side of the room. Said Wally, then: "Fred will take you. I'm not going just yet, Cass. Fred is just outside. Let Fred drive you home in the car and come back for me."

"Good God, man, I live two blocks away!"

Emmy Dale smiled up at him, one little hand at her throat. "Won't you come in again? Any afternoon. Tomorrow, maybe. There won't be so many people tomorrow."

"Sure," said Cass. "Thanks so much, Miss Dale . . . pleasure . . . picture . . . great success . . ."

He fled. The April twilight received him. He strode home through it, evading the patient Fred. Two rivers flowed through Park Avenue at this hour, an endless viscid stream. One was called Northbound Traffic and the other was called Southbound Traffic. Now and then these streams were checked by a Power with a single blazing eye, and at such times they parted like the Red Sea when it accommodated the Israelitish children, and the hordes from the east and west poured through.

Cass entered his own building. He let himself in with his latchkey. Lamps glowed softly in foyer and drawing room. The gleaming satin curtains were drawn, shutting out the city. Hilda was in her room, dressing.

"Darling, you're late."

"I stopped in at the Ambassador with Heavenrich."

She slipped her dress deftly over her head, shutting her lips in a tight straight line to avoid soiling the top of her corsage with the scarlet of her lip rouge. The dress was bouffant—a *robe de style* of taffeta and tulle. Cass thought her wise to wear it. Hilda's figure was a little inclined to the pear-shaped—narrow at the shoulders and disproportionately wide at the hips.

The dress hid these defects and gave her figure great elegance.

"I don't see why you go about with people like that."

"Wally's very amusing."

"So's the traffic cop at Fifty-seventh. But you wouldn't make a buddy of him."

"Why not!"

"Oh, you're in one of those moods. You're tired."

"I am not."

"All right, lamb. You're not. Did you have a hard day at the office?"

"About as usual."

"You know we're dining at seven sharp with the Geb——"

"I know, I know."

"Lie down for six minutes, won't you? You'll fall asleep in the middle of the second act if you don't."

"I don't fall asleep because I'm tired."

"Why then?"

He was fond of her. He couldn't say that he fell asleep because he was bored. So he said nothing. He kicked a satin chair, and Hilda said not a word in protest. He went into his room. The lamps were lighted there too, and his clothes were laid out.

Hilda was calling from her room. "It's quite a large dinner so there'll probably be two or three cars. Don't let that terrible Kassell girl get into ours when we go to the theater. And listen. Tell Jimmy I don't want to sit next to George at the show. Will you try to find out from Linda—she spills everything—what they paid for the place at Syosset? Remember to speak to Otto . . ."

He lay down across his bed and even closed his eyes. Miss Rosen would never have asked him to remember all those things. He breathed deeply. Scented air. Drawn curtains. Soft deferential footsteps. Low-pitched voices. Quiet. Luxurious. Shut in.

A prisoner until nine tomorrow morning.

THEY BROUGHT
THEIR WOMEN

EDNA FERBER

THEY BROUGHT THEIR WOMEN

1932

Edna Ferber

THEY BROUGHT THEIR WOMEN

MURIEL is a name you cannot trifle with. She herself was like that. Even her husband called her Muriel. It was queer about her. Her skin was so fair, her eyes so blue, her hair held such glints that unobservant strangers, dazzled by all that pink and white and gold, failed to notice her jaw line and the set of her thin red lips. They soon learned.

All the other youngish married women of her crowd were known by nicknames, or by cozy abbreviations—Bunny, Bee, Lil, Peg. Jeff Boyd's wife, Claire, actually was known to everyone as Hank Boyd, so that her own lovely name was almost forgotten. When first she had come, a bride, to Chicago's far South Side, Jeff had declaimed, "It's just a rag, a bone, and a hank of hair—a poor thing, but mine own." Hence Hank.

Then, as now, after nine years of marriage and two children, she was a skinny little thing; enormous brown eyes in a sallow pointed face; white teeth in a rare grin; a straight bob; a béret hung precariously over one ear; her fists jammed into the shapeless pockets of a leather jacket against the stiff Lake Michigan winds. She was

Hank Boyd to the whole crowd of steel-mill aristocracy living in the Chicago suburb that was a magic circle of green just within sight of the searing glare of the steel-mill chimneys—those stark chimneys bristling high above the slag-tortured Illinois prairie.

Muriel never called her Hank. She addressed her as Mrs. Boyd; or—somehow, it sounded even more formal—occasionally Claire. But Hank never called her anything but Mrs. Starrett. "It—it's the long *u*," she said once, in unconvincing explanation. "Funniest thing. I've struggled with it since childhood. I think I must have been marked, prenatally. I was sixteen before I could say funeral."

"Rilly!" said Muriel Starrett.

The two women, so nearly of an age, yet so unlike, probably never would have exchanged ten words had it not been for the friendship existing between their husbands. And that was strange, for the two men were as unlike as their wives. They had been classmates—Leonard Starrett the son of a South Chicago steel millionaire—Jeff Boyd, a pseudo-Socialist, working his way through the engineering course with the help of a scholarship.

Jeff was not one of your gloomy, portentous haranguers. Gay, red-headed, loud-voiced, free, he was possessed of a genius for friendship. He talked too much, he made execrable puns, he ramped and roared;

and was fundamentally sound as Marx himself, and ten times as charming.

The first thing that welded the friendship between the two men was an accidental look at a portfolio of drawings he had idly come across while waiting in Starrett's rooms at college. Leonard Starrett, entering hurriedly, late and apologetic, had found a red-faced and vociferous Boyd charging about the room, the drawings spread on every table, chair, cushion, and shelf.

"Listen. Whose are these?"

"They're mine."

"No, no, fathead! I mean, who did them! Who drew 'em!"

"I did."

"The hell you did!"

"Why not?"

"Say! Gosh!" He was so moved that Starrett was a little embarrassed.

They were drawings, in charcoal and in pencil, of steel-mill workers and their girls and their wives and their smoke-blackened dwellings. Hunkies. Bohemians, Poles, Hungarians, Czechs, Lithuanians, Negroes. There were men, stripped to the thighs, feeding the furnaces. You could see the muscles, like coiled pythons, writhing under the skin; smell the sweat; feel the strain of the eye sockets.

There were puddlers and rollers, in their shoddy store

clothes and their silk shirts, their yellow snub-nosed shoes and round haircuts, the Saturday-night cigar between their teeth, standing on the street corner watching the high-heeled girls switch by. The watchers' Slavic eyes were narrower still, their lips more sensually curled. Their shoulders threatened the seams of their ridiculous clothing. There were big-hipped women in shanty doorways, a child at the breast. Through the open door a glimpse of a man sprawled asleep on a cot, in his mill clothes, his mouth open, his limbs distorted in dreadful repose.

"Holy gosh!" said Jeff Boyd again, inadequately.

Leonard Starrett explained, politely. "That one I call The Boarder. Couple of rooms, family of seven, then they take in a boarder or two. Half of them work on the night shift and sleep in the beds during the day; the other half works the day shift and they use the beds at night. Neat little arrangement, what?"

"Say, listen, Len. Len, listen——"

"I call this one The Open Hearth, which isn't very bright of me because that's what it is. The big furnace where the stuff flows out white-hot. It's called the open hearth. One splash and you're burned through to the bone. It's exactly like a Doré picture of hell. I love the name of it. So cozy and homelike."

"You mean to tell me you been doing those things and never said a—— Why, say, Starrett, you've got to exhibit these, see! Exhibition of original drawings by Leonard Starrett. *Boy*, won't Prexy sit up!"

"Don't be dumb. I can't do that."

"Why can't you?"

"Can't."

"Now, listen. I don't know what I like, but I know about drawing. And you know's well as I do that these things are so good they're god-awful, so don't simper. Why, they're—they'll bust something wide open. You wait."

"I'm not simpering." He was gathering up the drawings and stacking them neatly into the portfolio. "My old man would have a stroke."

"Let him." Suddenly Jeff Boyd's high-colored boyish face grew thoughtful and almost stern. "What're you doing here, engineering and chemistry and slop, when you can draw like that, my God!"

"Oh, these are just—amuse myself."

"Amuse, hell! This is important stuff and you know it. What's the idea—Papa'll have a stroke."

Leonard Starrett hesitated a moment. Confidences came hard to him who had known a misunderstood childhood. He even looked a little sheepish.

"Uh—well, my father's a great guy but he's one of those from-the-ground-up boys. That's the way he began, and so that's the way he wanted me to start. Summers, since I was sixteen, I used to have one month in Europe and two months in the mills. Can you beat

it! That's how I began to draw. When the time came
for me to start here in the scientific end I got kind of
desperate and blabbed I wanted to go abroad and study.

"I showed him and my mother some sketches—these,
and some others. What a row! White hair in sorrow
to the grave, and all that stuff. So I agreed to come here
for four years, anyway, and learn to be a good little
steel official. Mother took me aside and explained that
if these things ever came to light they'd let Dad down
the toboggan. I guess they might, at that. He got in
early, of course, and made his pile, but he isn't one of
the big shots."

Jeff Boyd lowered his head pugnaciously. "I'll tell
you what. When you get through here, if your father's
got enough soaked away to live on—which you damn
well know he will have—and you don't go on drawing
and refuse to go into the mills if they won't let you
exhibit, I'll never speak to you again, so help me, for
a white-livered, sniveling this-and-that."

But Leonard Starrett did not exhibit, and Jeff broke
his oath, though the portfolio of drawings lay dusty
and neglected through the months, through the years.
For along came the war, and then along came Muriel,
and then along came Junior. The big steel mills became
monster mills, breathing fire and sulphur and gas over
the sand dunes, over the prairie, over the lake, so that
steel might be made wherewith Len and Jeff might kill

the Germans and the Germans might kill Len and Jeff.

But the two came back, miraculously, whole; Leonard to his father's steel mills and to Muriel—Muriel so strong, so enveloping, so misleadingly pink and white and gold, so terrible in her possessive love. And Jeff took a job there in the South Chicago mills, for there was the post-war disillusionment, and there was Hank. And Leonard Starrett went back and forth between the roar of the steel-mill offices and the quiet of his big house facing the lake. And the boy must have this and the boy must have that and the Whatnots are coming for dinner and bridge and oh darling what a lovely bracelet you shouldn't have done it.

Jeff Boyd was known as a brilliant engineer, but too quick on the trigger, and what's this about his palling around with the Bohunks? He sounds like a Red, or something. His name came up occasionally and uneasily at board meetings.

"There's nothing red about Jeff except his hair," Leonard Starrett would say, smiling. "You pay him less than men who are worth half as much to us as he is. He doesn't ask for a raise. The Youngstown people would grab him at double the salary if he'd go."

Muriel protested, too, the sharp edge of her dislike sheathed in the velvet of loving pretense.

"Darling, I don't know what you see in that Boyd."

"That's all right, Muriel. You needn't."

"But it is important, in a way, dear, because it's kind of embarrassing for me. If you're a friend of his, and ask him here, I have to invite his wife."

"Have to invite her! Why, everybody's crazy about her. She's a wonderful girl. Jeff says she"—he broke off—"and she runs that house with one maid, sees to the kids, and keeps her job at the Welfare Station three full days a week."

"I always say, welfare begins at home. I don't think those Boyd children look any too well cared for, if you ask me."

"They're not little Lord Fauntleroys, if that's what you mean." His tone was tinged with bitterness.

"Fauntleroy. You don't think I've made a Fauntleroy of Junior, do you?"

"You'll pin a lace collar and curls on him yet."

"You're not very kind, dear. But that's because you're not well. Goodness knows I'm not the sort of wife to come between her husband and his friends. But it does seem queer for you, whose father was one of the founders of the mills—they say the Boyds often have the Hunkies in, evenings, not for welfare work, but as friends—as social equals. They had four of the mill Negroes in to sing last week. Imagine!"

"Yeah, that's terrible. We met Robeson at Alice Longworth's in Washington last year."

"Oh, well, look at her father!"

"Yes. Low character he was."

"Darling, you hurt me very much when you talk like that, so bitterly. If you were really well you wouldn't do it. You couldn't."

It was a queer thing about Leonard's health. Muriel explained that he wasn't really ill. He was delicate. Not strong. The least thing upset him. That was why she never left him. When he traveled, she traveled with him. I've left Junior many a time when it almost broke my heart. But a wife's place is with her husband. Leonard comes first.

Jeff and Hank Boyd sometimes talked of it. "He was strong as an ox at college. Crew man, and out of training could drink beer like a Munich *Vereiner*."

"It's her," said Hank, earnest and ungrammatical. "She wants him to be sick so that she can have him all to herself."

"That," he agreed thoughtfully, "and not doing what he wants. He has hated the mills for—oh, almost twenty years, I suppose. I told you about the way he can draw —or could. Well, you take twenty years of frustration, and believe me you've got enough toxic poisoning in you to put you in a wheel chair."

"Can't we do something about her?"

"They hang you for murder in Illinois."

When the plan for the Mexican business trip first came up Muriel fought it like a tigress.

"Mexico! You simply can't go. I won't hear of it. Let them send somebody else. Why do you have to go?"

"Because we need what they've got, and because I think I can get it, and because we can't afford to overlook any bets these days and because the steel business, along with a lot of others, is, if I may coin a phrase, Mrs. Starrett, shot to hell-and-gone."

"That Boyd. Why are we taking that Boyd?"

He ignored the plural pronoun. "I'm taking Jeff because he speaks Spanish and because he knows more about manganese than any white man in North America and because he's a swell person to travel with."

"He won't be with us all the time, will he?"

"Now listen, Muriel. This is a trip you can't possibly take with me."

"But I'm going."

"It's impossible. Takes four nights and three days to get there, on the crack train. You don't know Mexico. The altitude's seventy-five hundred feet. It's in the tropics. The air's cool and the sun knocks you flat. They say it's dirtier than Italy before Mussolini, the food is terrible, you can't eat a thing, you can't drink the water, the country's full of typhoid and malaria and dysentery and lice and disease."

When she set her jaw like that he knew it was no use. "I can stand it better than you can. I'm stronger. I come of pioneer stock. If my great-grandmother could cross the country from New England to Illinois in a covered wagon, with Indians and drought and all sorts of hardship, and if *her* great-grandmother could come over the ocean from England . . .''

He had heard all this many times. So had everyone else. Muriel was very proud of her ancestry. Her family had been "old North Side." Her marriage to Leonard Starrett, which had brought her, perforce, to dwell on the despised South Side, amounted in itself to a pioneer pilgrimage. Muriel, fortunately, was all ignorant of the fact that, among the more ribald of the younger mill office set, she was known as The Covered Wagon.

Her overweening pride of ancestry had once caused even Hank Boyd to show a rare claw. It was at a dinner at the Starretts' and Muriel had been more queenly than usual. In evening clothes Muriel looked her best and Hank her worst. Hank was the cardigan type. Muriel was all creamy shoulders and snowy bosom and dimpled back and copper-gold wave and exquisite scent and lace over flesh-colored satin. Hank, in careless and unbecoming black, looked as if she had slipped the dress over her shoulders, run a comb through her hair, and called it a costume. Which she had.

Muriel's blue eyes were fixed on Hank. There were eight at dinner—four North Siders of cerulean corpuscles; the Boyds; Muriel and Leonard. "You can't

know what it means to one like myself, whose ancestors
—well, I'm afraid that sounds like boasting—but I
mean, when I read of all these dreadful new vulgar
people crowding in, getting their names on committees,
trying to push the fine old families out of their rightful
place!"

"Oh, but I do know," said Hank warmly. Her voice
was clear and light. "At least, I can imagine how my
ancestors must have felt."

"Your an——?"

"Yes indeedy. There they were, down at the dock
to welcome the *Mayflower* girlies when they stepped off
the boat onto Plymouth Rock."

Muriel allowed herself a cool smile as her contribution
to the shout that went up. Then, slowly, that smile
stiffened into something resembling a grimace of horror,
as the possible import of Hank's words was realized.
She stared, frozen, at the smiling impish face, the eyes so
deeply brown as to seem black, the straight black hair,
the dusky tint of the bosom above the crêpe of her gown.

"You don't—mean you've got Indian blood!"

"Only about one eighth, I'm afraid. My great-great-
grandpappy, they tell me, was old Mud-in-Your-Eye,
or approximately that."

It got round. Perhaps Starrett himself told it, or the
jovial Jeff. For days it enlivened South Side bridge
tables, dinner tables, golf games, office meetings. And

then she kind of stiffened and said, You don't mean you've got Indian blood!

Hank was a little ashamed of herself—but not much.

Leonard Starrett quietly went ahead with his preparations for the Mexican trip. So, less quietly, did Muriel. He might have uttered, simply, the truth. I don't want you. I want to be alone. Remember the man in *The Moon and Sixpence*. He did say something like this, finally, when it was too late.

"The firm won't pay your expenses, Muriel. This isn't a pleasure jaunt."

"Then I'll pay my own—if you won't pay them."

"How do I know how long I'll have to be down there! It may be a week, it may be a month. How about Junior? Planning to take him along too, I suppose."

"Mother'll move right in for as long as we need her."

"Remember the last time, when we came home from Europe? She'd darned near ruined him. Now listen, Muriel. I want to make this trip alone. I've taken a drawing room for Jeff and me from here to St. Louis, and from St. Louis on the Sunshine straight through to Mexico City. Please understand that Mexico is no tourist country, no matter what the ads say."

"I know more about it than you do," Muriel retorted. "I've been reading Gruening and Stuart Chase and Beals and all of them. I wouldn't let you go down there alone for a million dollars, with your indigestion and your colds and your——"

"Stop making an invalid of me, will you!" he shouted.

"There! You're a bundle of nerves."

"Oh——"

"What kind of clothes, I wonder. They say it's cool, evenings, and in the shade. Knitted things, I imagine, for daytime."

Defeat.

Hank Boyd, when she heard of it, flushed in deep rage—the slow, rare flush of the dark-skinned woman. "It's a rotten filthy shame, that's what it is."

"Oh, I won't let her bother me much."

"I wasn't thinking so much of you—you'll have an interesting time, no matter what. But poor Len."

"I wish you were going along, Hank."

"No, you don't, dolling. Thanks just the same. Though I've wanted all my life to see Mexico. Maybe, some day. Maybe it isn't as dazzling as they say it is. But Jeff, manganese or no manganese, find out all you can about the Indians; you know—if they're really as superb as I think they are, after the dirty deal Cortes gave them. Take a good look at the Riveras in Mexico City—and the ones at Cuernavaca, too. Find out if they pronounce Popocatepetl the way we were taught in school. Betcha dollar they don't. If you bring me home a serape I'll make you wear it to the office. Those things look terrible outside their native background. If there are any bandits or shooting, you run. I don't want no dead hero for a husband. I would relish one of those lumpy old gold Aztec necklaces, though I understand you have to tunnel a pyramid to get one. Don't touch water, except bottled . . ."

Hank and some of their friends came down to the train to bid Jeff good-bye. Two men and a girl. They were very cheerful. Muriel watched them from her drawing-room window as, at the last moment, they shouted to Jeff on the car platform.

"Good-bye, dolling!" Hank called, above the noise of departure. "Remember, drink three Bacardis for me the minute you strike Mexican soil."

"Don't do anything I wouldn't do!" From one of the men. Then they all roared, as at something exquisitely witty. Then the four of them, arm in arm, began to execute a little tap dance there on the station platform, chanting meanwhile a doggerel which—Jeff explained, later—Hank had made up at the farewell cocktail party.

Tap-tap-tappity-tap.

> "If you would live a life of ease,
> Go hunt the wary manganese,
> The manganese so shy and eke so docile.
> The manganese it aims to please,
> The thing to do is just to seize
> Upon it, be it fowl or fish or fossil.
> The manganese . . ."

The train moved; the quartet began to recede from view. Muriel and Len, at their window, caught just a glimpse of Hank's face, the smile wiped from it. One of the men tucked his hand under Hank's arm. They turned to go. The train sped through Chicago's hideous outskirts.

"Well," said Muriel, taking off her topcoat. "She didn't seem to be very broken-hearted."

Jeff appeared in the drawing-room doorway. He had a lower in the same car. His face was wreathed in smiles.

"What a gal!" he said. "What a kid!"

"I was just saying to Leonard, you two don't seem to be much cut up at parting." Her voice was playful, her eyes cold.

"The smile that hides a br-r-reaking heart." He glanced at his wrist watch. "Well, I'm going in and feed the featyures before the stampede begins. You people coming in, or is it too early for you?"

"We had an early dinner before we left at six," Leonard said.

Muriel took off her hat, began to open a suitcase, rang the bell for the porter. She was the kind of woman who starts housekeeping instantly she sets foot on a train. "I don't eat any more meals on a diner than I can possibly help. Miserable indigestible stuff."

Jeff laughed good-naturedly. "Ever since I could

afford it I've liked to eat on a train. You'd think I'd be cured of it by now. I guess it comes of having watched the trains go by, when I was a kid on the farm in Ohio, with all the grand people eating at tables with flowers and lamps. I thought it must be heaven to be able to do that. I always order things you only get on trains. You know—dining-car stuff. Individual chicken pie and planked shad and those figs with cream that come in a bottle, and deep-dish blueberry tart and pork chops with candied yams. It's never as good as it sounds, but I just won't learn."

Leonard laughed. "That's the way to travel."

"Doesn't it make you sick?" Muriel asked primly.

"Sick as a dawg. That's part of traveling. You can be careful at home." He was off down the car aisle, humming.

"Where's that porter!" Muriel demanded. "If a drawing room can't get service I'd like to know what can."

By the time Jeff returned from the diner she evidently had got the porter, for the drawing room was swathed in sheets like a mortuary chamber. Shrouded coats, like angry ghosts, leaped out at you from hooks. Books were neatly stacked, bottles stood on shelves, an apple sat primly on a plate, flanked by a knife; an open suit-case over which Muriel was busy revealed almost geometric contents.

Jeff stood surveying this domestic scene. "Len, didn't you break the news to Muriel?"

She turned from her housewifely tasks. "News? What!"

Jeff grinned. "We get off this train, you know, Muriel, at St. Louis, and take another whole entirely different train for Mexico City."

"This is nothing," Len replied for her, rather wearily. "Muriel puts up sash curtains and a rubber plant when she's in a telephone booth."

Muriel bridled. "I can't help it. I'm a home woman. And I'm not ashamed of it."

"You'd have a fit at the way Hank and I travel. But boy! Do we see things!"

Muriel sniffed. "We'll see you in the morning, Jeff."

"Say, what do you mean—morning! It's only eight-thirty. Come on back in the buffet car, Len. I met a fellow in the diner name of Shields. Lives in Mexico City. Knows the whole works. He says Mateos is square enough, but the Monterey outfit is crooked as a dog's hind leg. He's with the Universal people at San Luis Potosí. Quite a guy! He wants to meet you. Good idea, too, I think. Come on back."

"Now, Leonard, dear, you're going to do nothing of the kind. Sitting there smoking and drinking till all hours. You need a good night's sleep after the week you've had. You look perfectly haggard."

During the days and nights of steady travel that followed the change of trains at St. Louis, Jeff Boyd was up and down the length of the train and in and out of it at every stop of more than thirty seconds. He talked to passengers, conductor, waiters, porters, brakemen, and loungers at railway stations. He spoke Spanish, English, and bad German, as occasion demanded.

Muriel read and sewed. The scene in the Starrett drawing room was very domestic. Muriel kept the shades down about halfway, and a sheet across the windows because of the Texas glare and dust. She read books on Mexico. The very first day out of St. Louis, she had looked up from her book with a little exclamation. Then, leaning toward Len, she had pointed a triumphant finger at a paragraph.

"Listen to this, Leonard! Listen to what Gruening says." She began to read aloud.

"The diversity between the two cultures south and north of the Rio Grande is sharply discernible in the respective status of their women. *The North American settlers brought their women.* The squaw-man was outcast. The exalted position of woman in the American ideology dates from the pioneer days of companionate hardship and effort . . . The Aztec female, on the other hand, played the part of handmaiden to the warrior male."

She looked up, beaming. "There!"

Len looked about him, one eyebrow cocked a little,

as when he was amused. "A drawing room on a limited train may be your idea of companionate hardship and effort——"

He went back to his book. It was not a book on Mexico, but a slim little volume given him by Hank as a parting gift. Muriel had picked it up and looked at it. *Walden*, by David Henry Thoreau.

"Well, what in the world did she give you that for!"

He had wondered, too, at her choice of the plain chronicle of the man who had lived alone, in rigorous simplicity, at Walden Pond. He had opened the book, idly. He read a few pages. On page five he came to a line. Something shot straight to his heart, so that he jumped a little, as though he had been hit. Then he knew.

The mass of men lead lives of quiet desperation.

"You seem to be enjoying that book Mrs. Boyd gave you."

"Yes."

Every two or three hours Jeff charged in, bursting with facts valuable or fascinating or both. "That fat fellow with the fancy vest and one arm used to be the richest man in Mexico. They got him in the Revolution and 'did they take him for a ride! Burned down his hacienda, destroyed the crops, chopped up a couple of

daughters, shot his right arm off. . . . Next time the
conductor goes by get a load of him. He's Mex, named
Cordoba, wears a wing collar and a plaid tie with an
opal in it as big as your eye, and a gold cable watch
chain from here to here with a sixteen-peso gold piece
size of a dinner plate as a charm. . . . Say, Muriel, if
you'll take down that Turkish harem drape at the window and look at what's going by you'll learn more
about Mexico than from any book on Mexico—How to
Tell the Flora from the Fauna."

At San Antonio they had had an hour and a half.
The train drew in at eight. It would not leave until
half-past nine.

"Come on, folks. Let's shake a leg. Get some of the
train stiffness out of our bones. We can walk up into
town, take a look around, and beat it back in plenty
of time."

"Walk! At night! Through this district!"

Then it began in maddening futility. But what do
you want to ride for, Muriel, when we've been riding
for days? . . . Well, you two go and I'll just wait here.
. . . No, I wouldn't do that . . . But I don't mind being
here all alone at the station, really. I can just sit in the
train . . . A walk will do you good . . . Jeff, you walk
and Muriel and I will take a taxi . . . Good God, you
can't see anything in a taxi. Besides, the idea is the
walk . . . What is there to see? . . . Well, good gosh,

let's not stand here arguing, or none of us will be able to go . . . Leonard, this porter says it's a good mile and a half to the main street . . . Well, what if it is? . . . Now listen, fifteen minutes wasted . . .

After the train passed the border at Laredo and they were in Mexico, Leonard put down his book to stare out of the window, denuded now of Muriel's protecting sheet. She continued to read, placidly, while all the stark, cruel beauty of Mexico went by. The mesa; a cluster of adobe walls and huts, half-naked children, dogs, chickens, mules; cactus high as a man's head marching like an army of meager Indians across the desert; dusky women in pink petticoats and dark rebozos; swarthy men in dirty white pajamas, their unwashed powerful toes thrust into rope sandals; enormous straw sombreros, brilliant serapes flung across shoulders; withe fences; crumbling Spanish churches, pale pink and white and misty gray—and always, against the sky, purple at dusk, rose at sunrise, the Sierras.

"God, it's beautiful! I didn't know Mexico was so beautiful."

"Look at them!" Jeff exclaimed. "Look, Len. Those are the peons Rivera's been painting. Some magnificent, what! Makes you realize how darn good he is, doesn't it?"

Leonard Starrett said nothing.

"My, they're dirty!" Muriel exclaimed.

"That woman with the child slung in the rebozo and the jar balanced on her shoulder."

The hotel to which they went in Mexico City had been recommended because it was said to be clean and to have artesian well water. These turned out to be its only virtues. In all other respects it was like one of those fourth-rate little Paris hotels on the Left Bank in which the chambermaids run up and down the corridors on their heels, doors and windows slam, voices bellow or screech across the echoing court, and the mysterious custom of hurling what seems to be stove lids occurs every morning at five.

They could eat nothing there, though Muriel took her morning coffee and orange juice in her room. Len and Jeff breakfasted at Sanborn's, in the Avenida Madero. After three days of visiting other recommended restaurants, Muriel insisted on Sanborn's three times a day. In its American-Spanish patio hung with red velvet and bird cages she found, in all Mexico, the cleanliness, the familiar American language, and the creamed chicken, buttered beets, and apple pie to which she was accustomed.

"But this isn't Mexico," Len objected. "Might as well be eating at Childs. The other restaurants are full of people who seem healthy."

"'When you're in Rome——'" quoted Jeff.

Muriel was adamant. "At least you're not getting malaria and typhoid. Those other places are impossible."

Jeff said she had pleasantly condensed two hackneyed sayings to the single When You Are in Rome Do As the Romans Do, and Die.

Jeff bounded off alone. He tried them all—native restaurants, open-front cafés, cantinas and pulquerias —while Len accompanied Muriel drearily to Sanborn's. Jeff took a good deal of bicarb but he ate all the fearful native dishes, the frijoles, the enchiladas, the tortillas. "Hot dog! They burn the vitals to a cinder. Len, you got to taste *mole de guajolote*. Turkey cooked in twenty spices, any one of them guaranteed to eat a hole through asbestos." He even drank pulque. He insisted that they go with him for cocktails to a place he had discovered called Mac's Bar. He was enthusiastic about it. "Mac's an Irishman. He's lived in Mexico for forty years, without leaving it. He speaks of the United States as 'the old country.' Wait till you taste his Mac Special."

It turned out to be a dingy little vestibule of a place. Muriel said she certainly didn't think much of it. Jeff seemed a little chagrined and even bewildered. "I don't know. I guess I was wrong. I thought it was swell before. It doesn't seem like much. I guess it was just——"

They found time, during that first week, occupied though the two men were with their business, to make a short trip or two. They lunched well in the sun-drenched patio of the Inn at San Ángel, once a monastery. They drifted down the Xochimilco canals and came home with armloads of violets and roses. They whirled down the dusty roads across the plains to the Pyramids at San Juan Teotihuacán.

Leonard Starrett, long silent as he looked out at the Mexican countryside unfolding before their eyes, said slowly, "It's more mysterious than Egypt."

"Egypt's finished and done. This thing's just begun. You can feel the Indians boiling and seething underneath. Some day—bingo!"

Muriel looked about mildly. She was very careful to protect her fair skin from the straight rays of the Mexican sun. "Mysterious! Why, I was just thinking it looked a lot like the places outside of Los Angeles."

Muriel had a tiny camera, not more than four inches square. With it she took pictures of pyramids, mountains, rivers, cathedrals, and plazas. She had difficulty in pronouncing the Mexican names.

"Just call everything Ixcaxco," Jeff cheerfully advised her, "and let it go at that."

After a week Leonard came to her in some distress. "We're not geting anywhere. At least, we've just made a start. They don't do business here the way we do at home. They talk for hours. They only work about four hours a day. Jeff and I will have to be here a month, at least—maybe longer. I'd like to put you on the boat at Vera Cruz. They say it's a beautiful five-day trip. You'll land in New York, take the Century home, and we'll all be happier."

"I'm sorry my being here has made you and your friend unhappy."

"Oh, Muriel, for God's sake!"

"Please don't think I'm enjoying it. But I know what my duty is. And if you have to be here a month I'm going to look for an apartment."

"No!"

But for the next three days Jeff, stricken with dysentery, was wan and limp. That decided it. Muriel, with the aid of an agent, found an apartment in a good new building just off the magnificent Paseo de la Reforma. It was the apartment of some Americans named Sykes. He was a mining man. They were returning to the United States for three months. Mrs. Sykes showed Muriel all over the place. Very nicely furnished, and in good taste. A grand piano. There were even some good American antiques. A mahogany four-poster, a drop-leaf table, a fine old couch.

"These have been in the family for generations," Mrs. Sykes explained. "I'm very much attached to them. That's why I've never rented this apartment before, to strangers."

"I understand," Muriel said, with some hauteur. "I am a member and, in fact, an officer, of the Pioneer Daughters of Illinois."

"Oh, well, then," Mrs. Sykes said, reassured. She looked happily, pridefully, about her at her dear belongings. "You'd never know you were in Mexico, would you!"

Muriel repeated this to Leonard and to Jeff as she, in turn, showed them the apartment. You'd never know you were in Mexico.

"You certainly wouldn't," they both said; and roared with laughter.

"What's so funny about that?"

Mrs. Sykes had left her servants with Muriel. "They're very good," she had assured her. "As good as you can get—in Mexico. Jovita—the bigger one—she's rather handsome, don't you think?—is the cook. She's a—uh—I mean to say, she's a very good cook. She's used to having her own way. I wouldn't interfere with her if I were you." Then, as Muriel's eyebrows went up, "I mean, unless you're used to Indian ways—yes, she's Indian, and very proud of her ancestry—you might not understand. She does all the marketing."

"I always prefer to do my own marketing. It's the only way to get the freshest, the best. In Chicago——"

"But this isn't Chicago. Mexico is different. They

wouldn't understand. Another thing. You'll find she sometimes has one or two of her children here for a day or so. They're very quiet. She has four."

"Oh, she's married!"

"No."

"Oh, I understood you to say four——"

"Jovita has four children, of four different fathers. She has never married. She does not believe in marriage. She is the finest cook in Mexico City. She used to pose for artists. She is highly respected. I wouldn't part with her for the world. I'd rather not let the apartment, really, if you——"

Muriel related this to Len and Jeff, expecting from them masculine indignation. They seemed impressed, but not in the way she had expected. At their first dinner in the new apartment—Jeff dined with them— she saw the two men regarding Jovita, who assisted Lola in serving. The Indian girl, Jovita, bore herself magnificently. Her eyes were large and black; her skin a rich copper; her bosom deep, her shoulders superb, her hair straight, black, abundant.

"I really don't feel quite comfortable about Jovita," Muriel confided to the men, as they sat sipping their very good coffee, after dinner. "Having her here in the house, I mean."

"Well, I shouldn't think you would," Jeff agreed, with a great laugh. Muriel said, afterward, that she never realized how vulgar Jeff was, until the last two weeks. You really have to travel with people to know them.

Besides Jovita and Lola there was the Indian boy, Jesús. Muriel had objected to the name, but Mrs. Sykes had assured her that it was very common in Mexico among the Indians, and that he would be terribly offended if called by another name. The three servants were capable, quiet, and rather consistently dishonest about small things, according to American standards.

"Custom of the country," said Len. "Don't fuss about it. You're not going to live here. Take it as it comes."

"Jeff is always talking about how magnificent the Indians are, and how the race has survived in spite of everything, and how they'll rule some day. A lot he knows about it. If he can tell his precious Hank about her cousins the Indians I guess I can tell her a few things, myself."

Muriel was horrified to learn that Jovita usually slept on the floor of her little bedroom, rolled in her blanket, instead of on the very decent little cot bed provided for her. The boy, Jesús, had conceived an enormous and instant liking for Leonard. They discovered that he was in the habit of sleeping outside their bedroom door, like a faithful dog.

"I'd like to send them packing," said Muriel, again

and again. "The whole dreadful kit of them. Oh, how wonderful it will be to get back to my own lovely clean house, and to Junior, and to Katy and Ellen, and a good thick steak and sweet butter and fresh cream and waffles and a big devil's food cake with fudge icing."

They had asked Jeff to share the apartment with them, but he had declined, a little embarrassment in his high-colored boyish face.

"It's mighty nice of you to want me. But I think I'll just stay on at the hotel. I kind of like to bum around the restaurants and cafés and streets. I like to see the way the people live, and talk to them. But if you'll ask me to dinner once in a while I'll certainly appreciate it."

Muriel, with her fine fair skin, her coils of copper-gold hair, her plump, firm figure, attracted attention when she went out alone. She was accustomed, at home, to walking. All her Chicago friends walked for the good of their figures. She found that she almost always was followed home by some amorous Mexican.

Her admirer used always the same tactics. He would pass and repass her. He would double on his tracks. He would appear at unexpected and impossible corners. She would think she had evaded him. She would jump hurriedly into one of the crazy little Ford taxis marked Libre. But when she reached her own flat there he would be, miraculously, lounging against the building in his bright blue suit, his feet, in their American tan shoes, negligently crossed, a cigarette between his slim brown fingers.

She complained to Leonard and Jeff about this. "Horrid creatures!"

"Hank would get a kick out of that," Jeff grinned.

"I suppose she would."

"They don't mean anything," Leonard assured her. "It's the Latin way of showing admiration."

"They frighten me, the nasty leering things."

"Try taking Jovita along as bodyguard."

"Oh, well, if that's all you care. I don't understand you lately, Leonard."

"It's the altitude," fliply.

The servants made her nervous. They were in and out of the room without a sound. She would look up from a letter she was writing to find Jovita standing there, silent, waiting.

"Goodness, how you startled me. What is it?"

Jovita spoke very little English, understood a little, thanks to the Sykeses.

Jeff came to dinner two or three times a week. He and Jovita would speak together in Spanish. Suddenly Jovita's dusky impassive face would grow vivid with a flashing smile.

Muriel didn't like it. "What are they talking about?" she demanded of Leonard.

"He's going down to Milpa Alta on business Thursday. She heard us talking and caught the name. She's telling him it's her native village, where two of her children are. She says it's very beautiful, and that there is a festival down there next week—an important festival when everyone dresses up and there are fireworks and dances and big doings. Let's all go."

"Don't be foolish, Leonard. Those festivals are childish and stupid; the sun blazes down; you can't eat the filthy food, nor drink the water. You know it as well as I do. It's a mercy Jeff has been able to take the necessary business trips into the other districts. I'm glad, now, that you brought him along. I'd never have let you take them. Never. You would have, though, if I hadn't been here. You're like a child. Really, sometimes I think you need as much looking after as Junior."

"Yes," Len said thoughtfully. "I would have taken all those trips into the country, by motor and by mule, with the hot sun beating down by day and the cold coming on at night; sleeping, perhaps, on straw mats on the floor of some pueblo hut—if it hadn't been for you."

"Well, then! And the way Jeff looked last time. Remember? Though you can't tell me that was only the hardship of the trip."

Jeff was off to Milpa Alta. If this trip proved successful they could leave at the end of the week; the last, then, of their six weeks' stay. Jeff would be gone four days.

Next morning Jovita was not there. She simply was not there. No word, no explanation. Lola and Jesús shook their heads, spread their palms in innocent denial.

"I'll tell you what I think," said Muriel, with the abrupt coarseness of the good woman. "She's gone down there to be with Jeff, that's what I think."

"I hope so," said Leonard.

"What do you mean, Leonard Starrett!"

"I was just thinking."

"Thinking what?"

"I was just thinking how pleasant it would be to live for a year or two with Jovita in an old pink house, with a garden, in Cuernavaca, and paint pictures of the Indians, and of Jovita and her children, and sit in the sun, and in the evening, look at Popocatepetl and the Sleeping Woman against the sky."

"Leonard Starrett, have you gone crazy!"

"A little," said Leonard, "a little. But not enough."

NO FOOLIN'

EDNA FERBER

NO FOOLIN'

1931

Edna Ferber

NO FOOLIN'

As long as they were going to be stuck right there in Carlsbad, Mrs. Weeks said, for twenty-one whole days, they might as well buy Alice's trousseau linens. The windows of the linen shops on the Alte Wiese held her fascinated, writhing as they were with monograms, vine patterns, wreaths, curlicues, and hemstitching. There came a greedy glitter into Mrs. Weeks's eye, and her heart leaped in her housewifely breast. Dr. Goldschlagel had ruled that Father must stay for the full cure period of three weeks, with baths, waters, diet, packs, massage—everything.

"That gives us plenty of time to select. And even with the duty it'll come to much less than if we bought it at home. Such linen! And those monograms! They're like pictures."

Even a stranger might have remarked Alice's failure to meet this enthusiasm. George W. Weeks said, "A person would think this was your trousseau, Hattie, instead of Alice's."

So now you saw them marching up and down the

Alte Wiese, in and out of the linen shops, a little procession. Mrs. Weeks led, American woman fashion; plump, vigorous; Alice followed, cool, lovely, indifferent; George W. Weeks brought up the rear—gentle, shrewd, thinking his own thoughts. His face and his hair were the color of his good gray suit. When Mrs. Weeks noted that, it was as though a fiendish hand wrenched at her vitals.

The neat glistening stacks piled up, higher and higher: tablecloths, doilies, napkins, sheets, pillow slips, towels. Alice's monogram would afford a superb opportunity for the embroiderers' flourishes. "A. W. T." Alice Weeks Tuckerman.

"This diamond-shaped monogram with the vine pattern wreathed around it is the prettiest, don't you think, Alice? Or maybe the shield pattern is richer."

"Whatever you say, Mother."

"*I* say! Who's marrying Phil Tuckerman—you or me?"

"Mom, darling, you know I never was the girl to throw open a linen closet and gloat. I can't get emotional about tablecloths and sheets, I don't care how lumpy they are with initials."

"Well, girls are certainly funny nowadays." Mrs. Weeks would turn again to the white drifts piled high on the counter. "I think the twelve-inch napkins are plenty big enough for luncheon size, and then the great big ones for dinner. Jane's best ones are as big as luncheon cloths, nearly. Aren't they?"

Alice had drifted toward the doorway where her father stood gazing out into the colorful panorama of the winding street. She linked her arm through his. Mrs. Weeks's tone flashed a warning edge of impatience.

"What? What did you say, Mother?"

Mrs. Weeks now turned her full attention upon her spoiled daughter.

"Alice Corbin Weeks!" (Mrs. Weeks had been a Corbin.) "Now you listen to me. If you are going to cut up any of your monkeyshines you tell me right here and now. If you think your father can spend hundreds and hundreds and hundreds of dollars on linens, all monogrammed and everything, and then at the last minute have you change your mind again——"

"Oh, Mother! Really!"

But into Mrs. Weeks's memory had flashed the vision of her daughter's face as, two weeks ago, at the pier in New York, she had said farewell to the stricken and clinging Phil Tuckerman. Something then had warned Mama Weeks that no damsel, parting thus from her betrothed for two months, should present even to a watching world so unanguished an exterior.

She came over to the two in the doorway. Her voice vibrated with emotion. "Tons of tablecloths and sheets and everything, all ordered embroidered in A. W. T.

You're not a child. Changing your mind all the time. My land, you're twenty-three!"

George W. Weeks's interest in the matter of linens and monograms was less than negligible. American husband and father, he was required to be concerned in such matters only at the check-book stage. Papa Weeks was something of a darling. There were strata in his make-up that Mrs. Weeks had never penetrated; of which she was, indeed, completely unaware.

His gray face now crinkled in a little secret smile. "'Put it down a we,' Hattie. 'Put it down a we.'"

But Hattie Weeks did not care for Dickens, and had never heard of Tony Weller. "I don't know what you're talking about, George. Some of your nonsense." Yet, curiously enough, her next utterance unconsciously carried out her husband's cryptic suggestion.

"Do you know what? I've a good notion to have all the monogramming done in your initials. Some people do. Brides, in the old days, with hope chests. Just A. C. W. I swear, if I had to go back to New York with all this linen and then have somebody pick the *T* out of everything, it would just about kill me."

Alice now drew herself up to her full height—five feet one and a half. "Please, Mother. You make me feel so—cheap." She turned to the bewildered Austrian saleswoman. "A. W. T."

The woman bowed a little, and smiled a little, and

nodded her head a good deal. "These Americans!" she thought. *"Gott im Himmel!"*

Certainly there was some excuse for Mrs. Weeks's perturbation. Though things had never before actually reached the embroidered-monogram stage, Alice Weeks had, since her eighteenth birthday, been engaged to a procession of Phil Tuckermans. She was now twenty-three. Twenty-five, a warning milestone, was clearly to be seen up the road.

Her girl friends, back home in New York, had married, for good or for evil, and were even beginning to be bored with the novelty of their own apartments furnished with wedding gifts after the style of their day. It was the year 1912, and their bridal nooks were modish with mahogany or oak library tables, overstuffed chairs, sectional bookcases, Tiffany-glass lamps. Alice's two brothers, George Junior and Hobart, had married, and their Jane and Lillian had already presented them, respectively, with a daughter and a son.

Alice, the family agreed, was fickle and frivolous and spoiled. These accusations Alice vainly denied. She sensed, though she did not know clearly, that in her seeming capriciousness lay a genuine constancy. She became engaged to marry; she broke the engagement.

She could not clearly explain, even to herself, that each time she thought, in her willingness, in her eagerness to find love, that this was it—this was the perfect thing. Each time she had found that what she, in her rashness, had thought to be real was only a substitute; and she had refused to accept second-best. The family joked about it. "You ought to issue rain checks, Allie."

Only her father had not ridiculed her. "It's all right, Allie. You be as sure as you can. Of course you can't be sure. But you've got to think you are, anyway."

He spoiled her. Everybody spoiled her. Her father treated her as though she were a little girl, her brothers as though she were a rather annoying princess, according to the habit of American fathers and brothers. It was not her fault, certainly, that she had a heart-shaped face, eyes like animated pansies, and golden curls such as you saw on the magazine covers that Christy was making so popular. In view of all this, the beholder naturally overlooked her square jaw and the firmness of the lips.

Then, too, her lack of height gave her an enormous advantage over the tall and broad-shouldered American male. Almost always she was obliged to look up at the person with whom she was speaking. This lent her a misleadingly melting look, and she thus was frequently surprised and even enraged to find herself suddenly swept into the great arms of a six-foot acquaintance to whom she was merely being politely attentive.

Thus equipped (or handicapped) she had gone her imperious way. Phil Tuckerman, a baffled fiancé, had rebelled in vain at her announced intention to spend two months in Europe with her parents. "But I do, Phil, really I do. I've told you over and over. And it's only for two months. I've never been to Europe, and goodness knows if I'll ever get another chance, and I've always been dying to go, and as long as there's that wonderful Dr. Goldschlagel, or whatever it is, in Carlsbad, and everyone tells Dad the cure there is absolutely what he needs, and after that we're going to Vienna and to Budapest and to Paris. Paris! Why——"

"Just the same," muttered Phil Tuckerman darkly, "just the same, if you really . . ."

Mrs. Weeks thought so, too, in private conversation with her husband. "Just the same," as though continuing a chant, "just the same, when I was engaged to you, if anyone had tried to make me go away for two months before we were married they'd have had to drag me by main force."

"Girls are different now. Alice is different."

"Girls aren't. Alice is."

So they were in Europe together, the three of them, and George Weeks was saying amiably, "Well, now, what do you girls want to do, huh? Whatever you say."

They always knew, and told him. It scarcely ever was what he wanted to do. He never thought of rebelling. The ladies, God bless 'em.

Carlsbad seemed to turn the trick. "But you won't

feel the real benefit until next winter," Goldschlagel had said. "This cure is really a Christmas present." They thought that was a very original way of putting it until they discovered that all the Carlsbad doctors said the same thing to discharged cure patients.

When they reached Paris the two women shopped relentlessly, for Father Weeks had business of his own. George Weeks, in New York, had to do with stocks and bonds, and his European trip was not wholly in pursuit of health and pleasure. "Now I've got to see these fellows at the bank. You girls run along and enjoy yourselves."

Sometimes at dinner with his wife and daughter he let fall upon their inattentive ears some fragmentary account of his day's doings. "Dusty, old-fashioned holes they've got for business. But smart! We think we're smart, in New York. Say, we're babies." He was thinking aloud, really. The women were not interested.

At his next words, however, they gave him their attention. "You girls meet me for lunch tomorrow, will you? I've invited Delage, of the Crédit International, and Tellier, his assistant. You see, they're kind of the French connection of our New York office. Like to show them a little attention."

George Weeks was not a New Yorker, born and bred. He had come East from the Middle West. His would always be the homely vernacular of his native region.

Alice Weeks said, "My French is terrible, and I don't think the Frenchmen are a bit good-looking."

"They speak English better than you do, young lady. And you're not expected to marry them. They're married, for all I know, so you can concentrate on your lunch and think about Phil, but be polite, will you, because this is kind of business."

Delage, chief of the investment department of the Crédit International, did turn out to be married; the rather snuffy type of pre-war Paris professional or business man, with a long parchment face, striped trousers, black coat, badly fitting collar. But Paul Tellier was different. Paul Tellier was so different that he took Alice Weeks's whole life as you take a piece of shapeless cloth, and fashioned it into the pattern he thought best for her.

He not only had been married, he was a widower, childless, and almost ten years older than Alice. He was tall, thin, incredibly graceful in speech and movements. His eyes, dark brown and velvety, would have been too soft and fine had they not possessed the saving and hardening alloy of intelligence.

He was nearly bald. This, in some curious way, only added to his attractiveness. He looked, Alice thought, like a young diplomat. She had never seen a diplomat, old or young. He spoke English perfectly, but with a little accent that made his most commonplace remark sound altogether enchanting.

She had extended her hand for the firm clasp with which one greeted new acquaintances back home. He brought it to his lips and lightly kissed it. He looked down at her. Alice Weeks, in the past five years, had been kissed on the lips, the eyelids, the back of the neck, the throat, the shoulder. No one had ever kissed her hand in that impersonal, magnificent, and altogether satisfactory way.

It made her feel more powerful, more helpless, more feminine than she had ever felt before. Phil Tuckerman's kisses faded into the limbo of such unadult delights as ice-cream cones, matinées, country-club dances, and orchids. Her protracted adolescence fell from her like an ill-fitting garment, and she stepped forth in that instant a woman.

They were married. This was irregular and unusual, for Paul Tellier came of upper-middle-class French people. These, unlike the lower class or the nobility, both of which frequently lapse, almost invariably marry of their own. They were deeply in love. Seeing this, George and Hattie Weeks were alarmed, then really frightened.

"But you can't marry a Frenchman and live in France. Frenchmen are different. They're not like

American husbands. You're engaged to Phil. Are you going on like this all your life?"

"No. No. No."

"You'll march yourself on that boat, young lady. It's the same thing all over again. You'll forget him before we're out of Plymouth Harbor." So they sailed according to schedule.

But when Mrs. Weeks saw her daughter's face as she parted from Paul at sailing she remembered how Alice had looked on leaving Phil Tuckerman in New York two months before. She knew, then, and resigned herself to the inevitable. This was the face of a woman terribly and passionately in love.

"I guess this is the real thing this time," George W. Weeks said. "Kind of tough on Phil, but anyway, Hattie, your *T* is safe on all those sheets and stuff."

Paul came to New York in September. They were married. Back they went to France. The girls all agreed that Paul was distinguished-looking, but not at all the type they had expected Alice to marry.

Alice had five thousand a year from her doting father. Paul's salary at the bank was almost four thousand a year, and another thousand or so inherited from his parents and his late wife. They could live in Paris comfortably, even luxuriously, on these combined sums.

They took an apartment in Passy, very Parisian, with big high-ceilinged rooms and handsome chandeliers, parquetry floors and no hot water from July until September.

Their child was born a year later. They named him after his American grandfather, spelling it "Georges," in the French fashion. This, to his American relatives, by a process of family joking, and to avoid confusion, became "Gorgeous," and as Gorgeous they always spoke of him.

The Tellier apartment was furnished with care and taste. Paul had some excellent things of his own; Alice's wedding gifts had been liberally sprinkled with family checks. The pieces they bought were very French in the old manner, calculated to last a lifetime, and beyond. The apartment in Passy, and its furnishings, remained the same throughout the nineteen years of the Telliers' married life.

"*Planter le chou*," Paul said. "To plant the cabbage," literally, but really an expression of the aim of every middle-class Frenchman. To put aside enough for a permanent house and a piece of ground in the country, there to live in serenity in one's later years.

When Mr. and Mrs. Weeks came again to France for a first look at their new grandchild they gazed with amazement upon their erstwhile spoiled darling. France, the most material, the most thrifty, the most adult nation in the world, had absorbed her and made her its own.

"Well, Paul, you certainly have made a woman of our little girl," Mrs. Weeks said sentimentally.

"Are not all little girls potential women?" Paul replied, rather pleased with his neatness.

Paul Tellier was head of his household. Alice Tellier had soon learned that the French husband is always head of his household, and that the French woman rules by indirection. The result, she discovered, was much the same as that achieved at home by the more ruthless and less femininely diplomatic American woman.

At home, in New York, her father had been only the nominal head of the household; Mrs. Weeks always had ruled with a heavy hand. In her brothers' households George Junior and Hobart lived in a sort of pleasant subjection to their Jane and Lillian. These American wives decided where to go for the summer holidays; which people to invite for dinner; the schools to which their children were sent; the furnishings of the house; their husbands' very ties, shirts, pajamas, and even suit patterns.

All these things Paul Tellier decided, but Alice influenced that decision by suggestion. This, too, she had early learned. Paul engaged the servants, chose the furniture, selected a tutor for Georges, said the pictures were to be hung there and there, approved Alice's clothes, supervised the food and its cost. Yet behind all these decisions was Alice, who, perhaps through love, had learned tact and adaptability.

"It's such a lovely tapestry, Paul. Where do you think it should be hung? I suppose you'll decide on a place not too near the big picture there, and yet where it will get the proper light so as to bring out the colors."

"We shall hang the tapestry just there."

"Are you sure?"

"It is the one proper place for it."

It was hung. They surveyed it. "Oh, Paul, how right you are! It's perfect there. You always know."

It had been hung exactly where she had wanted it hung.

Their friends were French. Some of these things she had learned from them, for she was young and quick and intelligent and in love. It seemed that all Frenchwomen did as she did, and so they were a great power in the land. Every Frenchman was a Louis, and beside each was a Maintenon, guiding, suggesting, ever so delicately and persistently.

This diplomat, this statesman, this financier, this artist, all gently and with exquisite tact advised and swayed and influenced by the hard, unsentimental, straight-thinking brain of a French woman. So the French men kept their manhood and their self-esteem and the French women kept their powerful feminine wiles and each was busy and content.

Sometimes, with a kind of unbelief, Alice recalled her young married friends back home, and her brothers and sisters-in-law.

"Bart, get four seats for a show tomorrow night. Bob and Helen are coming to dinner. Their bridge is impossible and I won't just sit and talk."

"That's a terrible tie. You do have the rottenest taste. You look as if you were going to a Polish wedding."

"I'm going to have the couch re-covered in green. Called up the upholsterer today. It'll be one seventy-five."

"Next spring I'm going to have our room done in peach."

"I'm going to apply at Lawrenceville for Peter."

"She's awful. If you want to talk business with him then ask him to lunch or out to the club or something. I won't have her here."

"Let's go to California for a month. Stell says it's lovely in the summer. I'm sick of Massachusetts."

In those first two years of her married life, from 1912 to 1914, Alice Weeks grew to be more French than the French. From the first, Paul had spoken her name in the French fashion, the second syllable stressed, the *i* given the long *e* sound. She had become Alice Tellier, through and through.

After Paul had come home from the bank that July

day, white-faced, and had taken off his business suit, which he was not again to put on for four nightmare years, there came many frantic cabled messages from Mother and Father Weeks in New York.

"Come home. Come home immediately."

"I am home," she had cabled, in reply.

The French soldiers, unprepared, in ridiculous bright red pants and bright blue coats went scurrying in taxi-cabs to meet the olive-drab horde just outside the gates of their beloved Paris, and thereafter, for four years. Alice Tellier lived in an exciting kind of hell. If she had failed to become completely adult in the past two years, certainly these next four accomplished it. Some-times, as she walked up the Champs Elysées toward home in the late afternoon, with the Arc de Triomphe etched in grandeur against the sunset sky, she thought of America, of New York, dimly, fondly, as one re-members a childhood game, a schoolday sweetheart.

One slight arm wound, a brief period in hospital, Paul was back in it again. A second wound, almost at the close of the war, in the leg this time, a long business; not crippled, but he would limp a little for life. He came home.

Delage, his chief in the investment department at the bank, had not been so lucky. The striped trousers and the black coat and the frumpy collar had been laid aside forever. Paul stepped into his place as chief. He had seven thousand a year, now, as salary. A man of forty-odd, resembling in his dress and manner the American business man of his own age and class.

They had changed much, in many outward aspects, the French. The comic-cartoon Parisian, with the black spade beard, the baggy trousers, the dramatic shoulders, the gesticulating hands, seemed, somehow, to have vanished in the trenches, never to reappear. Except for that tiny blood-red spot of ribbon in his buttonhole, Paul might have been any American business man.

"*Planter le chou.*"

So they bought a house near Mantes, in Normandy, about seventy miles from Paris. They went there in the summer. The flat in Passy remained unchanged. There was a cook, Marcelle, and her husband, Léon, houseman-chauffeur, for the Telliers had a small car of their own now. Little Georges had a tutor at home. When he was eight he would go off to the Ecole des Roches, forty miles from Paris.

Georges learned to ride, and to fence, and to play tennis, and to speak German and English as well as his native tongue. They had a tennis court at the place in Normandy. Léon tended the small grounds and the really fine rose garden.

"We'll raise our own vegetables," Alice had said at first, making one of her few mistakes.

"Oh, no," Paul had answered. People in their class

did not raise vegetables. It simply was not done. The very rich, with large estates, grew their own vegetables, and the peasant class, but not the middle class. It would have been beneath Léon's dignity to attend to vegetables. Roses were all right. He could care for a rose garden with propriety. Unwritten French rules.

It was in 1921, when Georges was eight, that Alice Tellier went home for her first visit since her marriage. Her father, she thought, looked ill and old. Things bewildered her, shocked her. There was about everything a vast and careless lavishness.

To her eye, accustomed to the post-war frugalities of Europe, the splendor all about her was Roman, was barbaric. The very streets seemed to be flowing with food; fruit stands were bursting with richness; every stenographer wore a fur coat and silk stockings glisteningly new; fat, glittering motorcars choked the streets; twenty-five a seat for the Follies; a dress seen in a window on Madison Avenue and bought as casually as though it were a handkerchief.

At home, in Paris, Alice had a new evening dress every year, a new dinner frock, a street costume, all well made. Throughout the winter she saw her friends, and they her, again and again in the same costume.

She spoke of these things to her father, feeling a little frightened and breathless. "Everybody's got too much of everything. Or perhaps it's just that I'm not used——"

He had smiled grimly. "Going to be an awful yelp when the piper comes around."

All the changes, too, bewildered her. Things had changed kaleidoscopically. All her friends had moved again. Everything, everyone, had moved. All the furnishings of the apartments of her sisters-in-law and her parents and all her friends had been whisked away—had vanished—and things of a completely different sort had taken their place. Buildings had changed, whole streets, districts, even.

"Oh, now, Alice. This is a young, vigorous country. We're a vital people. We don't sit in one place all our lives. Don't be so snooty and superior and old world."

"I'm not. I didn't mean to be. I'm just not—doesn't it make you tired to get used to new things like that, all the time? Adjusting yourself constantly. Like a fresh shock every little while."

"Oh, say, listen!"

"I just mean it's so comfortable to have things where you expect them to be."

The visit wasn't much of a success. Everyone spoiled Gorgeous. He seemed very quiet and a little pale and even puny compared with the amazing precociousness of his young cousins; their physical development, their boundless vitality. There were Bill, young Bart, Ernie, and Sally (quaint names had come in for girls). Besides, he was, they thought privately, too pretty for a boy, having inherited Alice's curls and small-boned frame.

Little Gorgeous and his Grandpa Weeks became great friends. Curiously enough, they did not talk very much when together. "Gorgeous is such a quiet child, Allie," the family said. "Is he always quiet like that?"

"He isn't especially quiet. French children are different. They're different from American children."

"French! Oh, yes, I suppose he—seems funny, for a minute, your saying French children."

"Anyway," Hattie Weeks said, as bustling as ever, "I don't think a good tonic would do that child a mite of harm. I'd take him to Walsh and see what he says. Anæmic, I'll bet."

"Leave the boy alone," George W. Weeks said, in his mild voice. "He's all right. He's different. He's not a rampager, like the others."

He looked down at the boy. Gorgeous looked up at him. At that instant there was, between the sick old man and the young child, a striking resemblance; a fleeting thing, more of the spirit than of the body.

"He looks like you, Father," Alice said suddenly.

"Fiddlesticks! He's the image of you," snapped Hattie Weeks.

George Weeks put a slow hand, with its skin so dry and splotched with brown spots, on the golden head of the eight-year-old boy. "No. It's just that we think alike about things, I guess." A strange statement.

She went back home to France with relief, with joy. The dear family figure, with its little limp, there on the pier at Havre. The flat at Passy, unchanged. The house at Mantes, unchanged. Marcelle, Léon, the same.

Five years went by, eight, nine. Always short, she had grown a little plumper. She must be careful. Marcelle cooked too well. Still, none of this starving such as her sisters-in-law in America practised. She was so French by now that the tourists who thronged the Paris streets in the late spring and early summer, before the family went to Normandy to stay until autumn, seemed to her eyes almost as strange and alien as to the native Parisian; their dress, their walk, their voices, their gestures.

"Well, look, you and Gert go do your shopping and I'm beating it back to the hotel. . . . What'll I get for Aunt Gussie? I got to bring her something. . . . Some place where I could get a real good cup of coffee. . . . Lookit that cop. Say, the guy corner Forty-second and Fifth could eat that frog for a gumdrop."

The Telliers had survived the war. France had survived the war. The decade marched to its end. Paul Tellier the same—suave, charming, assured, older, certainly. In another ten years, perhaps, there would be enough, and he would step down to make way for a younger man. Alice, still pretty, still youthful-looking, though the forties were upon her; the long-lasting youthfulness of the small woman blessed with good eyes and skin and hair.

The two lived the quiet, serene, well-ordered life of their class. But underneath there was a difference. Perhaps that difference lay in the boy, Georges. He had been brought up as millions of French boys before him had been brought up. But there was about him something not easily explained.

He was almost eighteen. There was about all the French boys of his generation that same inexplicable difference. It was as though, in the period between 1914 and 1924, a whole generation had been skipped, and these boys were decades ahead of their time.

Georges was still too beautiful. His hair was too soft and curling, his skin too fine, his hands and feet too delicate. It was a fragility he had inherited from his mother. Strangers were misled by it. The lad was normal, male, intelligent, aware. He was more than this. About him, and the other boys from eighteen to twenty-five, there was an uncanny composure. The pre-war frenzy had preceded them; the post-war bewilderment had found them too young. But they had felt the shock and the after-effects of both these periods, and now you saw them looking about, cool, wise, seeing.

Theirs was a curious adult hardness. They were like metal that has been through a furnace and has come out resilient, but harder, more powerful than when it went in. It was uncanny to see them as they surveyed a writhing and tortured world. Adages by which their fathers had lived were rendered ridiculous. "As solid as the Bank of England." "I could no more do that than fly." "As good as wheat."

Meaningless phrases now.

You've made a fine mess of it, they seemed to say to their elders. You and your sayings. Don't think we don't know.

It was as though civilization itself were in the balance, and upon them depended the outcome. They played games, they flirted, they sulked, laughed, loved, as generations before them had done. But the look of awareness was in their eyes. The young of France, the young of Germany, the young of England, world-conscious, for the first time in the history of the world.

The market in America, that had been performing breath-taking stunts high in the sky, now collapsed in a nose dive. Mrs. George W. Weeks took the tumble very badly indeed. All of America took it very badly indeed. For a moment it stared, open-mouthed, dumb, eyes popping. Then it began to scream and scramble.

Mrs. Weeks screamed and scrambled. Elevator boys and policemen, millionaires, actresses, stenographers, grocery boys, doctors, policemen, lawyers, Negro porters, shoe clerks, business men screamed and scrambled. Their money. Their money was gone. Where?

Someone must have it. There was a mythical monster named They; and They had it.

Mrs. Weeks wrote frantic letters, which had been preceded by still more frantic cables.

Your father's income is hardly a third of what it was. Goodness knows what will become of us all. I'll probably never be able to come to Europe again, so if you want to see your father and mother you'll have to come here, that's all . . . The money your father slaved for all his life just blown away . . . Your father is a very sick man . . .

The Telliers, in France, felt it, too. Calmly they arranged themselves. The house at Mantes was their own now, paid for. Georges was to enter the Polytechnique. He would be an engineer. Nothing must interfere with that. They would let nothing interfere.

Still, even the French cannot fight Fate. Paul Tellier, on business connected with the bond department of his bank, booked passage on the big ten-passenger plane to Berlin. Three hours later, broken and charred, so that twisted metal and twisted human flesh were alike unrecognizable, the plane lay a blot in the middle of a neat German field planted thriftily with spring vegetables. Wild little figures, their arms waving, sprang out of what had seemed to be deserted countryside and ran toward the blazing pyre, and then stood helpless, shielding their faces.

Alice Tellier's eldest brother came over from New

York. He attended to things. He was very kind. "Now look here, Allie. No use you and Gorgeous living here in Paris any more. Thing to do is to settle up everything here and come on back home. We're all broke, but we can be broke together. You and Gorgeous can take an apartment with Mother and Dad. Gorgeous can go to Boston Tech or Cornell or Harvard."

"I want to stay here. Georges wouldn't be happy— the house—Paul wouldn't have wanted us to——"

"Now, listen. Your home's America. Gorgeous has had about enough of France, anyway, I'd say. Do him good to mix with the kids at home. Bring him back to the good old U. S. A. where he'll get around with two-fisted guys with hair on their chests."

"I want to stay here. We want to stay here."

"On what? You could just scrape Gorgeous through his engineering, and that's about all. The house at Mantes is clear, all right. But there's precious little besides. You can't sit out there, alone."

She made a last desperate stand. "I don't want to be a burden. The depression over there. Mother's letters are always—and the girls', too. Lillian and Jane always write—and the racketeers and the drinking, and the noise and the——"

"Well, I certainly am ashamed of you, Alice Weeks. Your own country. The finest country that God ever . . ."

She and Georges sailed in June for America. The flat in Passy was dismantled and left forever. She had kept the house at Mantes. "Until the autumn," she said. "Until I know. How do I know?" Her pretty face was white and stricken.

Léon and Marcelle went out to the house at Mantes, as usual, and Léon began placidly to attend the roses, and Marcelle to buy and conserve fruits and berries as they came along—enormous strawberries the size of plums, and enormous raspberries the size of strawberries, and enormous currants the size of raspberries.

Unexpectedly enough, Gorgeous was eager to go, thrilled at the prospect. He had been in Germany; he had been in England. He knew German boys, and English. "I want to see what they're doing. Everything's upside down there. It will be fun to see what they are doing about it. It will be important. I want to know what Bill thinks, and Bart, and Ernie."

They took small cabins on an obscure deck of an unimportant boat, but it was a French boat, and Paul Tellier had been a man of standing in his quiet way. They were given every courtesy, every attention.

Georges was enormously interested, more excited than she had ever seen him. He talked with everyone. He walked the deck with Americans and with the French and talked and asked innumerable questions. Alice knew a growing terror of America, of her mother, of her brothers, of their wives, Lil and Jane, and of their two-fisted sons with hair on their chests.

The Paris winter had been the usual Paris winter, intensified. Cold, with a penetrating cold from which there was no escape; gray, heavy, damp. The sky, for weeks at a time, was like a dirty canopy of wet gray cotton. The trip across the ocean was a succession of just such gray wet days.

Then, suddenly, on the morning of their arrival, they awoke at Quarantine to brilliant June sunshine. Scarlet-funneled ships on a blue bay lay bathed in golden sunshine. The air was clear, was brilliant. And suddenly Alice Tellier felt light, happy, almost gay for the first time in many weeks. They came majestically up the river. She felt American and a little hysterical as she stood at the rail with Gorgeous.

"Look! Oh, look at that one. That must be the Empire State. Look, Georges! Everything looks sort of pink. Rose color. It's beautiful. I didn't realize. It's been ten years."

The boy stood looking. It was curious, the look on his face. He had looked like that when they had put him, a small boy, on a horse for his first riding lesson. Frightened; determined not to show it.

At the tip end of the pier was an enormous bouquet

that resolved itself into faces and hats and gay-colored frocks and waving handkerchiefs. Lil, Jane, Bart, Hattie.

"*Dar*-ling! How *won*-derful you look! You look simply *mar*-velous. *Gor*-geous, *how* you've grown! Isn't he *hand*-some! Look, he's blushing. The boys couldn't come down. Big lazy things. They won't get up during vacation. Well, darling, how *are* you? You look *stun*-ning in black. Doesn't she, Mother? Bart, tend to the trunks. Bart, you know that man who's one of the inspectors or something. Get him to hustle Allie's things through. Now, go *on!*"

They were all so kind, so solicitous, so genuinely eager to make her comfortable. They all had dinner with Mother and Father—the whole family. It was lovely, but a little overpowering, too, after the journey, the rush, the excitement.

The boys, Bill and young Bart and Ernie, were stupendous enough to be an event in themselves, not to speak of the rest of the family. They looked amazingly alike; or perhaps this was due to their height, their breadth, their astounding color and vitality. Two-fisted guys, with hair on their chests. Compared with them Gorgeous seemed colorless, almost insignificant.

"H'are you, Gorgeous?" they said. Took his hand in their enormous grasp.

George W. Weeks was a shrunken old man. Alice

was wrung with anguish as she looked at him. "Well, Dad, here's your wayward dotter back."

The Depression. The talk at dinner was of the Depression. They joked about it a good deal. Gorgeous began to ask questions. Alice almost wished he wouldn't. He was so eager, and the boys—Bill and young Bart and Ernie—seemed so offhand and big and careless. "Say, what you birds in Europe lack is the light touch. Everything's on the toboggan. What the hell!"

It was the same when they had dinner at Lil's, next night, and at Jane's, the night following.

"Is this true? Is that true? What is being done about this and that?" Georges would say. He was terribly in earnest, and a little cuckoo, they thought.

"Call up Hoover," they would say, to his mystification.

He was tiresome, with his questions, with his theories. He would hold forth. Young Bart would say, "No kiddin'." It was an expression uttered with the falling inflection, and contained no hint of interest. Rather, it expressed a bored sophistication.

Certainly Georges's phrases were not new; all Europe had mouthed them until they were frayed and shabby. But there were no others. The boy was terribly in earnest and deeply interested in what he saw, and they wished to Gawd he'd shut up.

"Vitality of America all that is left . . . eyes of Europe

. . . end of western civilization unless . . . crime . . .
Prohibition . . . Communism . . . world credit . . .
only the young can help . . ."

"No foolin'," said Bill, yawning.

"Get a soap box," said young Bart.

"Yeah!" said Ernie.

Alice and Georges had dinner at Jane's, at Lil's.
They had again moved into new apartments, both.
In the first ten days since coming to New York, Alice
could not recall having seen them in the same dress
twice. They talked a great deal about the depression.
This Depression, they said, as though it were an individual they hated.

Their furnishings were new. The details bewildered
Alice. The hall closets and clothes closets were painted
in brilliant colors, and hung with satins or chintzes.
The shelves were edged with frills or pleatings. They
looked like the tiny boudoirs of midget harlots.

"This one is done in Chinese," Lil would say, quite
seriously, and open a closet door to reveal a riot of
lacquer-red and orange and green, with Bart's somber
masculine garments, or big Ernie's, hanging incongru-
ously in its midst.

The bathrooms. Alice Tellier had forgotten about the
lavish luxury of American bathrooms. Rose bathrooms,
jade-green bathrooms, delft-blue bathrooms, modernistic bathrooms. On the side of the wall in each was a roll

of paper, and that, too, was rose or blue or jade-green to match the tilings, the rugs, the shower curtains.

Gorgeous had burst into shouts of laughter at sight of this. His Gallic sense of humor had been tickled. Jane and Lil were a little offended at his lack of delicacy. "Haven't had anything new in ages," they said. "This Depression. I wanted to have the apartment done over in modernistic, but I suppose I'll have to wait to see how Things turn out."

Bill and Bart and Ernie all advised Gorgeous to go to Harvard. "Harvard's got the team this year," they said.

Gorgeous had seen that they scarcely glanced first at a newspaper's front page, with its stories of a world trembling on the brink of dissolution. England. Russia. Germany. India. Italy. Japan. China. Turmoil. Chaos.

Straightway they turned to the sport sheet.

"Schultzy got a homer, a double and two singles off Weblin in the first."

"Yeah, but the Giants got it cinched with McGork."

"Who says so?"

"I say so."

"No kiddin'."

At the end of two weeks Alice said, "Oh, Georges, you can't judge people. You're too young and too ignorant of the ways of the country." They were speaking French, as they always did when alone together.

"Yeah?" said Georges, not without malice.

"This is a new world—not old and tired, like France. They're like children. Like beautiful, charming children."

"That isn't it at all," said the strange boy, Georges. "They talk and act like children, but I have been listening and they are bitter and disillusioned and they don't care any more, and that is why I think it is no use here. They are soft, from these last fifteen years. The first blow has felled them."

"Oh, Georges, you're really behaving like a terrible little prig. You go around looking so superior. Your father used to look that way, sometimes, after he had had a conference with an American business client. It always annoyed me, I don't know why, much as I loved France."

The boy was bewildered. He took to going about alone. He made amazing discoveries. He talked to his grandfather about what he had observed, for George W. Weeks alone of all the family seemed to find these items remarkable, or even interesting. The boy was very excited. He walked up and down the room as he talked. The old man sat in the wheel chair to which he was now bound.

"It's all very gay," the boy finished up, breathlessly, "and terribly exciting, you know, and you have to run like everything. But I'm so confused. No one ever does or says anything that I'm expecting them to do or say. Why is that?"

"Young folks, you mean? Or everybody?"

"Everybody. Everybody except you."

The old man, with his fingers clasped, chased his two thumbs one round the other, round and round. "That word they are all so slick with—psychology. Well, tell you, Gorgeous, it's a funny psychology—that of this country of ours. Of mine. We're still simpering and giggling, with a finger in our mouth, and saying, 'Oh, we're such a young, young country.' Reminds me of a skittish old maid. We used to be a young and wild and headstrong country. But that's past now, or should be. That was finished fifty years ago. I kind of wish America would be its age."

Georges went to his mother.

"I have talked to Grandfather," the boy said.

"Yes," Alice said absently. "That's nice. You are sweet to Grandpa, dear. The boys never seem to talk to him, really. Sitting there, all day."

The boys always came in, big, glowing, rather overpowering. "Hello, Gramp! H'are you? Hello, George W. Weeks, old socks! How's the boy?" Very hearty. They never really talked with him.

"I have talked to Grandfather," Georges Tellier said again, slowly. Something in his tone made her look at him, then, attentively. And in that instant his voice sounded so like that of Paul Tellier, his whole aspect was so terribly that of his dead father, so little did he resemble his mother, whose very form and features he had, that Alice Tellier knew a moment of actual terror. "Hear me." He spoke rapidly, in French. "We are leaving America. We will sail for home next Tuesday, on the *Paris*."

"We can't."

"We will."

She felt helpless. She was shocked into helplessness. But glad, too. Glad. "Georges! Do you mean it?"

"No foolin'," said Gorgeous grimly.

KEEP IT HOLY
EDNA FERBER

KEEP IT HOLY

1933

Edna Ferber

KEEP IT HOLY

Sᴜɴᴅᴀʏꜱ were the worst. There were the evenings during the week, of course, but they weren't so terrible. An evening comes to an end. By the time she had eaten her dinner and read the tabloid and perhaps gone to a movie it was ten or after. There were always Things To Do, evenings; stockings to mend, gloves to wash, a dress to press, a letter to write, hair to shampoo, nails to manicure. Then, too, you are tired and sleepy after stitching hats all day, and trying them on customers' heads, and rushing them through for delivery. But Sunday! Sundays stretched endless hours ahead. You got nowhere. They were like a bad dream in which you walk and walk and make no progress.

This was her third Sunday in New York. You couldn't count that first Sunday because she had gone back home to Hartford for that. Well, she knew better, now. She closed her eyes as though to shut out the memory of that first Sunday when she had gone back home to Hartford to see the folks.

As she lay in bed now, on Sunday morning, at ten

o'clock of a brilliant February New York day, she said to herself, as she often had said in the past four weeks, Linny Mashek, you're a lucky girl to be in New York and have a good job and do what you want to. Having told herself this, firmly, she stared hard at a modernistic pattern sketched brightly on the ceiling by the bold spring sunshine, and began to cry. So then she sat up in bed, looking very plain indeed, and remarked, aloud, "You need a good cup of hot coffee, that's what you need."

Luck had played a small part in the drama that had landed her in New York. She knew nothing of that. She knew nothing of the letter which had lifted her out of Hartford, Connecticut, and deposited her in Miss Kitchell's millinery shop on upper Madison Avenue, and in this rooming-house bedroom (five dollars a week and no cooking allowed but everyone knew that didn't mean coffee).

DEAR KITCH,

Well, I'm married to a Hunky up here in the sticks believe it or not. He owns a nice house and a Buick here in Hartford and a tobacco farm about ten miles out with an old farmhouse on it like you see pictures in the magazines I'm going to fix it up quaint later. Maybe I was a fool but I don't think so. I was good and tired of working and anyway things the way they are a person is lucky to have a home and I'm no spring chicken any more. When I came up here to take charge of this hick millinery department last fall I never dreamed I'd end up living here. He's Polish extraction and real good looking his wife was a Swede died a year ago. He has got two sons married to Polack wives live near by but I can settle their hash all right. I put on my little black Lanvin copy and talk New Yawk and they run like I had hoofs and horns. But look there is a girl too a dead loss lives at home unmarried and probably always will be. And that is where you come in, Kitch. Her name is Linny—Linny Mashek. I am Mrs. Mashek now can you beat it. I asked her what do you mean Linny and she said that was short for Linne or even Linnaeus he was a Swede botanist discovered something about flowers and her Swede mother was crazy about flowers always raising them in the yard and named her after him is that goofy or isn't it I ask you. Well anyway Kitch here is my proposition. Now listen Kitch. This Linny is an A 1 milliner. I know because she worked under me here and has got natural style and knack and an eye for line. They laid her off here with others because business is terrible the factories all shut down and the boobs not buying hats and I guess they will go back to shawls if this keeps on. She lays around the house all day and I am going crazy. She worshipped her Swede ma. She is twenty-three looks more though she is little. The way I met her pa was she asked me to come to the house for supper one Sunday night they had schnapps and beer and goose and fixings you'd be surprised the way these Hunkies live. Well, this Linny is as smart a milliner as I ever worked with I'm telling you straight. A girl with her eye for line and copying would stand you forty a week in New York even in these times. She can copy anything and original too I don't know where she gets it. She can do them on the head, too. She'll work for twenty a week. I will send you three weeks wages that is sixty dollars and you will have an A 1 worker in the busy spring season won't cost you a red cent for three weeks. After that if you want to keep her its your own lookout but if I once get her out of the house she stays out. I don't mean I am a mean stepmother or anything but the way she mops around the house and looks at me drives me crazy. Do this little thing for me will you Kitch you won't lose by it. She isn't a bad little thing quiet and homely but not a bad egg. I have done many a favor for you in the past and you know it. Me and my old man will probably be driving down to New York in March in the Buick when the weather gets milder and I'll be seeing you. Now do this will you Kitch for old time sakes.

Your old pal Tessie.
MRS. GUS MASHEK
(Couldn't you die)!

Miss Kitchell, Millinery, Hats Made On The Head, sold guaranteed copies of French models at five to seven dollars. Miss Kitchell had unvenerable white hair, a basalt eye, and a black-clad figure which was the battleground on which Miss Kitchell's strong will waged perpetual war against the flesh. Miss Kitchell's voice, firm yet furry, was lifted hour upon hour in phrases that had become a chant through repetition.

This just came in . . . You can't tell a thing in the hand . . . I love it on you . . . More over the eye . . . It's a little Suzanne Talbot . . . It's a little Rose Descat . . . It's a little Reboux . . . This just came in . . . I love it on you . . . More over the eye . . . You can't tell a thing in . . .

In the littered workroom behind the showroom Linny Mashek stitched and folded and steamed and pressed and cut. It's promised for tonight it's promised for tonight it's promised for tonight.

At the close of the first bewildering week Miss Kit-

chell, glancing sharply and not unkindly at the girl's
white face and twitching hands, had said, "Well, thank
God even Saturdays come to an end. Listen, Mashek.
If I was you I'd catch myself a good rest in bed all to-
morrow morning and then go out and see New York.
You got some friends here?"

"No," said Linny. "No."

"Well, you'll soon make friends. Anyway, there's
lots to interest a young girl in New York. There's the
Metropolitan Museum and the Natural History Museum and the Aquarium and the Bronx Zoo. A person,"
concluded Miss Kitchell, "can live here in New York
all their life and not see the half of it."

"I think," said Linny, "I'll go up home this Sunday
see the folks and come back on the late train Sunday
night."

"Don't do that!"

Linny was a little startled at the vehemence of Miss
Kitchell's tone. "Why not?"

"It's foolish. What do you want to go and spend your
money like that for? Why'n't you stay here in New
York and see the sights?"

"I will, next week. I guess I'm kind of lonely for—
for—not lonely exactly, but I just thought I'd run up
home and see the folks. I wrote a letter Thursday and
told them I was coming, just for Sunday. Anyway, I
want to bring back a couple of things. Little things I

didn't bring when I first came, like a picture of my—of my folks, and some things like that."

Miss Kitchell shrugged her shoulders in a gesture of resignation.

"You tell your—you tell Mrs. Mashek I said you'd be better off staying here having a good time seeing the sights."

"I'll tell her," said Linny, mystified but polite. "She'll be glad to hear from you."

"Oh, my God!" exclaimed Miss Kitchell.

Well, Linny knew better now. She had come home to a closed house at Hartford. Everything closed tight. Doors locked, windows locked, shades pulled down. She rang, knocked, pounded. The cellar door locked, the garage door locked, even the back pantry window that had never had a lock before. They had gone to the farm, most likely, for the day. They had never got her letter and they had gone out to the farm for Sunday.

At the rear of the house, in a last foray before going to her brother's, her eye was caught by the stunted old apple tree whose bare limbs just reached the roof of the back porch. She smiled then, a wide grin of delight. A childhood spent with two older brothers had taught her a trick to foil locked doors and downstairs windows. She took off her good Sunday coat and her smart new hat and placed them on the back porch steps, with her gloves and bag neatly on top. With a swift glance around she tucked her skirt about her belt and was up the tree, onto the flat roof of the porch like a cat, and through the second-story window. It was fun. She would tell the boys about it, later. The back hall was dark. She dusted off her hands, pulled down her skirt, opened the hall door, and came face to face with her stepmother.

They stared at each other. Their opening words sounded like the dialogue in a bad translation of a Chekov play.

"My! A new hat!"

"It was locked. You locked it!"

"Your pa's at the farm."

Well, she knew better now.

On the second Saturday, at closing, "Miss Kitchell, what do you think is the most interesting thing to see in the Metropolitan Museum, to start with?"

"Well, I've never really been. I meant to go a million times. But Sundays I'm so dead I'm glad to be off my feet, let alone tramping around looking at pictures and like that. Weekdays I'd look swell, wouldn't I, running to museums with a living to make!"

That first New York Sunday she had awakened to rain. The rain had turned to a soggy snow. The combination had formed a slush that made galoshes a necessity. Still she had started out with an almost gay feeling of adventure. Anything might happen. The movies had taught her that Romance, in the person of lithe young men with cleft chins and quizzical eyebrows, roamed the parks, the streets of New York. Later in the day she decided that Romance was blighted by galoshes and an umbrella. Certainly the start had not been propitious. She was not certain about the location of the Metropolitan Museum. Fifth Avenue in the Eighties somewhere. Coming from her rooming house she stood a moment at the corner of Lexington and Eighty-sixth. Fifth Avenue was over there—uh—no—over—let me see. A man with his coat collar turned up and a cigarette dangling limply from a corner of his lips was standing slouched in the doorway of the cigar store. Not a young man; shabby, with pimples. A man.

"I beg your pardon—" that was the way you approached strangers in Hartford— "I beg your pardon, but could you tell me—is that the way to the Metropolitan Museum?"

"The what?"

"The Metropolitan Museum on Fifth Avenue."

"Not today, sister," the man said.

She walked away, her chin up. He could have given her a civil answer to a civil question. Making fun of her like that. It didn't even make sense. Not today. Through there was the park. She could see the bare branches of the trees. That was Fifth Avenue. It must be right there, somewhere, the Metropolitan Museum.

She was wearing a brown coat with a good fox fur

collar, and a nice little hat she had made herself; and excellent gloves and stockings, and neat pumps beneath the galoshes. Everything she had on was good and modish, in the manner of the American working girl. She had added a tiny veil, for coquettishness, but it was not right. Her sharp nose poked it out, and a black dot in the wrong place gave one eye a drooping look. She was short and very slight, but her smallness had not the appealing and miniature quality that endears babies and kittens, and that arouses the protective instinct. It was, rather, a meagerness, as though nature had skimped.

Up the broad steps of the vast edifice. Check your umbrella here. The great marble halls of the Metropolitan were swarming with people, for the day was cold and wet and gray.

She stood alone in the center of the huge entrance hall. She looked up at the stairway ahead. She glanced to the right, to the left. Things Egyptian leered at her. Undraped Greeks in athletic poses stared at her with sightless marble eyes. Mythological monsters yawned in her face.

Everyone seemed to be there in couples, in families, or in hordes. Italian families of five or six children, all strangely of a size, regarded the statuary with the accustomed gaze of people to whom Michael Angelo's David is a thing you see always in the piazza on market days. They dragged themselves over miles of floor, past endless walls glowing with the blues and crimsons of holy groups and the mild moon-faces of Neapolitan madonnas. The boys were in full regalia of American kiddie-clothes. Their swimming Italian eyes looked out from beneath hat-bands on which were printed in gold letters U.S.S.Minnewaska. The husband, in his Sunday blacks, seemed to shrink and fade into the background. The woman always held a lunging lump of a child in her arms. Staring eyes and pendulous cheeks, he hung perilously over her shoulder to peer into glass cases containing aristocratic Tang figures with disdainful evasive faces.

"I bet she isn't any older than I am," Linny thought. "And look at her. All those kids, and no more shape than our cow back home. I wouldn't change places with her." And then, "I bet she don't know what lonesome is, all those kids squawking."

The place was remote, in spite of the swarms, and overpowering. It's real inter*est*ing, though, she reminded herself. In one of the picture galleries she stopped before an Inness; a valley bathed in golden light. It made her think of Connecticut, in the autumn, back in the hills. It made her happy to look at it, but a sad happiness. Since last week—since last Sunday— she had had a curiously heavy feeling—a feeling of uncertainty. She had experienced, crudely and ruthlessly,

the sensation of not being wanted. It had shaken the
very core of her self-confidence. She did not know this.
She only felt it in some obscure and painful way.

Sargent's portrait of Mme. X, a figure of great elegance in her black velvet with its tiny waist and swelling
hips and bosom. Her cold passionate profile was turned
away from the girl staring up at her. Snooty old thing,
Linny thought. Chase's devilish portrait of Whistler
she passed with a blank gaze. Rembrandt's Old Lady
Cutting Her Nails. Degas's ballet girls with their muscular legs and distorted feet. Well, what did people want
to go and paint things like that for!

People whispered. They tiptoed and whispered. Linny
found herself tiptoeing, too. She went up to a guard
(elderly) and whispered. "It says the American Wing."

"Second corridor straight ahead turn to your left
turn to your right turn to your left turn to——"

"Thank you so much," said Linny. "I'm ever so
much obliged." Miraculously she found it, but it seemed
to her to be poor stuff. They had as good as that in the
farm attic back home, stuck away in dusty corners.
Stuff that had been there years, long before Pa had
bought the old place. And old tables, scarred and hacked
like the chopping block in Vogelsang's butcher shop in
Hartford. A placard said 1650–1675.

Cool court ladies done in ivory miniatures framed in
jewels and resting on velvet. Do Not Lean On The

Glass. Twelfth Century Armor. Brocades. Mummies.

"Oh, fine!" said Linny, next day, in answer to Miss Kitchell's question. "There's so much to see you can't see it all in one day."

"It's a wonderful city, New York is. People who live here don't half appreciate it."

The pimply man on the cigar-store corner was sometimes lounging there, evenings, when she came home from the movies or from work. She passed the corner on her way to her room in Eighty-sixth. "Hello, sister!" She turned her head away, disdainfully, like that picture of the woman in the black velvet at the Metropolitan. The old fool, as if anybody would want to speak to him.

It was funny, though. A week would go by and she would have spoken to no one except Miss Kitchell and the customers whose hats she fitted in the shop. Only women and women. Never a man. You couldn't count Florida Cream, the colored errand boy who swept, and delivered the hats and brought materials up from the wholesale district. He slapped about in a torn red sweater and shapeless cap and fringed pants. But he must have a large social life of his own, after hours. There had been, one night, some confusion about the promised delivery of a hat, with hysterics on the part of the customer. Linny had been summoned from her rooming house and Florida Cream from Harlem. He had appeared in such a blaze of pinch-waist French blue topcoat and fawn-topped shoes and yellow stick and pearl gray fedora as to leave her gasping.

She remembered a Hartford girl she knew who had gone to New York to work in a beauty parlor. That was over a year ago. Emma Hovak. On her rare visits back to Hartford, Emma had been all fur-trimmed coat, glinting hair, trough-like wave, and scarlet nails. Linny searched her memory for the name of the beauty parlor. She called Emma Hovak.

"Hel-lo!" said Emma, summoned to the telephone. The expectant note in her voice amounted almost to a trill. Linny had not given her name.

"This is Linny."

"Who?"

"Linny Mashek."

"I guess you got the wrong party."

"No. Linny Mashek, from Hartford. Linny Mashek."

"Oh. Oh, hello." It was another word altogether, that hello. A silence. "You down for the day?"

"I'm living here in New York. I'm working here."

"Yeah?"

"I thought—what're you doing—I mean I thought we could fix up a date for next Sunday, maybe——"

"Listen, Linny, I'm all dated up for Sunday. This Sunday and the Sunday after and—I'll give you a ring, see. Listen, I got a client, see, I'm giving her a henna she'll have a fit we're not supposed to answer the telephone when we're doing a henna. Listen, I'll give you a ring real soon——"

She had not even asked where Linny worked or lived.

That third Sunday had been one of those piercingly brilliant New York days, blue and gold and sharp. She had slept late, and then, awakened by the sunshine, she had prepared her own good breakfast—the coffee she loved, and coffee cake and a surreptitious egg, and a slice of ham bought at the delicatessen the night before. Sustained and almost happy, for the coffee had been strong and the day was bright and she was twenty-three, she strolled across Central Park toward the Natural History Museum. Florida Cream had told her something of the wonders it contained.

"Animals," he had said, his eyes rolling, "called denasserusses, bigger than any elephants you ever see used to roam the earth, one lick of their tail would knock down a tree; and Indians, stuffed, and tigers and mete-rites fell down from the sky as big as this here room. Boy! I sure hate get hit by one them!"

Groups of girls and groups of boys and Sunday fathers with their offspring, pompous and a little bored. And couples and couples and couples. The couples had cameras. The girl was forever taking a snapshot of the boy or the boy of the girl, accompanied by giggling, pouting, and general coquetting on the part of the girl and embarrassed comedy from the boy.

"Aw, Merton, stand still and straighten your hat, woncha! Lookit how you look, your face."

"Well, can I help it if you don't like my face! It's the only face I got." Salvos of laughter rewarded this bit of repartee. There were young men, alone, on park benches in the cold sunshine, but there was nothing relaxed and indolent about their lolling. They had the look of this year's young men to whom park benches were no luxury. Linny glanced at them, shyly. Their gaze was blank; or it slid past her, unheld.

There was a pleasant informality about the crowds that swarmed the Natural History Museum. They had nothing of the stiffness and rather puzzled awe of last week's Metropolitan Museum hordes, made self-conscious by supercilious Gainsboroughs and nude Greeks. Small boys raced the aisles, pointing pop-eyed at monsters and snakes and tepees. Still smaller boys said, "Lift me up, Pa!"

"It's only a canoe a Indian canoe says sea-going war canoe of the—uh—Haida Indians live on the coast of Alaska——"

"I wanna see in! I wanna see in! Lift me up!"

Linny liked the giant trees; the California sequoias, enormous blocks of wood grown for centuries, for a thousand years, as large in circumference as a room. "Lookit! Ut's a tree!" The small boys pointed, scuttled on.

Middle-aged couples stood together before glass-enclosed exhibits, their faces upturned in the pure expression of learning. For the moment they had the eager receptive look of children. They stood, boy and girl fashion, the man's arm loosely about the woman's broad waist. His hand rested on her hip; thick spatulate fingers with work-stained nails—rather touching in their Sunday idleness. He read aloud from the placard, being the learned of the two. "The Struggle for Existence. Every human thing, plant or animal, is engaged in an unconscious struggle for existence with other living things. In order to live, the Meadow Mouse must be able to escape its enemies such as the cat, the skunk, weasel, hawk, owl, and snake. It is the survival of the fittest——"

The two stood gazing with new respect and understanding at the family of Meadow Mice in the glass case. Meadow Mice themselves, that waist and that broad hand, struggling for existence against the skunk, the weasel, the hawk, the snake.

Two nuns in their anachronistic garb bent their wimpled heads over a chaste display of waxen blossoms under glass; Color Inheritance In The Flower Of The Four O'clock, Red And White. Above the delicate petals of the four o'clocks was a small portrait of a man in priest's garb, a cross upon his breast. Gregor Johann Mendel, discoverer of the Mendelian Law of Heredity.

"Cute," said the younger of the two black-shrouded figures, with a last glance at the four o'clocks. They turned toward the case showing the evolution of the polliwog.

Glyptodonts, mammoths, dinosaurs. Tyrannosaurus Rex. The largest flesh-eater of all times. The Alaskan moose. Peninsular giant bear. Florida panther. The American bison. The tsine or banting. Sumatran rhinoceros. Forest, river, and ocean life. Linny found herself sidling into groups, in order to hear them speak. Once a couple glanced at her over their shoulders and moved on, pointedly annoyed. She felt her face get hot.

"You getting acquainted with New York?" Miss Kitchell asked, on Monday.

"Oh, yes."

"It don't take long. First thing you know you'll be a real New Yorker. I ought to get out more, Sundays. I'm so dead I do my sight-seeing in bed, with the papers. Time I get myself pulled together it's six and some of the crowd begins coming in."

Now, on this fourth Sunday, as she lay in bed staring at the pattern of sunshine on the wall, these things went through her head, not in orderly fashion but disconnectedly, in pictures and flashes. Her father now fifty-three, a zestful fellow with a stocky muscular body and a dark ruddy skin and iron gray in his hair. He was better-looking now than when he had married the

Swedish girl who had worked with him on the farm a quarter of a century ago. His new wife's face. Linny did not even call her stepmother in her mind. The shop. Miss Kitchell. Hartford Sunday. Portrait of Mme. X. Not today, sister. It's a little Suzanne Talbot. Lift me up, Pa. The American Wing 1650. I'm dated up this Sunday and next Sunday I'll give you a ring sometime, see. Then some of the crowd begins coming in.

It was then that she had begun to cry, her face screwing up absurdly. It was after that that she had said, aloud, to herself, "You need a good cup of hot coffee, that's what you need."

She rather enjoyed these Sunday breakfasts, after the weekday morning scramble and gulp. She had two meals only on Sunday—her leisurely coffee and bakery coffee cake and her egg when it was nearly noon; her dinner at the Werner cafeteria at six. She drank a great deal of coffee, a habit inherited, perhaps, from her Swedish mother. There always had been a pot of the strong brew simmering on the stove back home.

This five-dollar room was not sordid or uncomfortable. It was small and not very bright. Most of the furniture had some minor disability—a chair rung missing, a knob broken, a caster off, a mirror crazed. But the landlady had learned about cretonne, and the one window caught briefly the late morning sun.

Peering out, after breakfast, Linny was aware of

something odd in the air—something different. She
felt it when she stuck her head out of the window, but
it did not penetrate her room or the dank subway.

The mazes of the Sunday subway bewildered her.
There were no guards in sight. The whole thing seemed
to function without human aid. Trains rushed into
stations, unguided. Doors opened and shut mysteri-
ously. People were spewed forth, others flowed in, the
train fled into the black cavern. There was no one of
whom to ask a question. New York assumed that, having come, you knew your way about. If not, you could
damn well find it. Linny plucked up courage to ask
direction of middle-aged family men with wives. There
were young men, too, in gray fedoras and belted overcoats and gay mufflers, but Linny was too shy to ap-
proach these. After the rush of boarding the train the
passengers, seated or standing, fell into a kind of
catalepsy, staring glassy-eyed before them or up at the
advertising placards overhead. They did not speak.
Couples sat sedately, their eyes sliding round. There was
color and life, though, in the smart Negro girls resplendent in fine red or green cloth coats with big fur collars
framing the flashing vivacity of their faces. Their
chocolate cheeks were delicately rouged, enhancing the
liquid brightness of their eyes. Occasionally, when a
door rolled open, there tumbled in a laughing jostling
group of boys and girls. They carried the inevitable

camera. They never could find seats all together. They
called across to one another and made personal jokes,
shoving, nudging, giggling. Linny sat regarding these
with an expression which she intended as a blending of
hauteur with contemptuous amusement. She envied
them.

Once out of the subway at the end of the line, walking
through Battery Park on her way to the Aquarium,
Linny knew, suddenly, the name of the thing that had
vaguely troubled her when she had stuck her head out
of the bedroom window to sniff the air.

It was spring.

There in Battery Park, for the first time since coming
to New York, she had a feeling of freedom, of exhilaration, and of peace. All that blue sky, all that tossing
bay, all those clouds, white and puffy, the scarlet funnels of the ships; that vast bank of towering buildings
left behind, like a prison wall from which you have
escaped.

Peanuts! Popcorn! Crackerjack! Chocolate bars!
Pretzels! Everyone seemed to be eating something.
Jaws worked rhythmically. Gum. Apples. Bananas.
Linny bought a bag of peanuts and entered the close-
smelling circular hall of the Aquarium. At once she was
caught up in the fascination of the unknown and unusual and fantastic. She followed the crowd, munching
her peanuts, staring, held. With the rest she pressed

against the rail above the circular pool. It held cormorants. They stepped about, stiff-kneed, mincing. Linny was puzzled by their resemblance to someone she knew. One cormorant in particular—the biggest one. Its craw hung down like a double chin. It stuck out in front and it stuck out behind. It looked about with a cold and bawdy eye. It bridled and leered and minced, elegantly. It had a way of ducking the head and drawing in the chin, with horrible coquetry. Its unvenerable white head was close-clipped and neat.

"Miss Kitchell, of course!" said Linny, aloud. She blushed with embarrassment then, but the Sunday crowd did not heed her.

As Linny became accustomed to the dim green light of the room she saw that it was infested with bleary bums asleep on benches tucked around the supporting pillars—scabrous gentlemen with a peculiar bluish cast to the skin and loose open mouths. Defeat had stamped her iron heel on their faces, distorting their features into strange lumps and depressions. All about them, in pale sparkling tanks of water, glass-enclosed, flashed brilliant living things—orange and scarlet and jade and lavender things. They were like no fish she had ever seen. Rather, they seemed orchids endowed with the power of locomotion. In another tank a vast fleshy thing waggled majestically up to the very confines of the glass wall and stared superciliously at the gaping crowd outside like a fat dowager gazing with lackluster fishy eye through the plate-glass window of her limousine.

On one of the little circular seats a blond boy lay asleep. His clothes proclaimed him a sailor from one of the battleships anchored up the Hudson. A sailor on a busman's holiday, visiting the Battery and the Aquarium. As he lounged there, relaxed in slumber, his huge hands were open and defenseless. His head had fallen on his breast. His shock of yellow hair was like a pompon. He was, perhaps, twenty. Childlike and helpless, there in sleep. Linny Mashek, looking at him, suddenly longed to sit beside him and very gently place her body so that the yellow pompon should be pillowed on her breast. The impulse was so strong as to frighten her. Abruptly she turned away, pushed through the crowd massed in front of the tank containing the sea horses— miniature monsters, and unbelievable, like something out of *Alice In Wonderland*. Just ahead of her stood a boy and a girl. Under the guise of gallant attention the boy touched the girl whenever possible. He helped make way for her through the crowd toward the tank, protected her from the crowd, again made way out of it, and always his hands touched her—her shoulder, her arm, her waist, her hip—mutely wooing her. The girl wasn't pretty. She wore eyeglasses. Linny hated her. She walked behind the two, toward the doorway. In a niche in the wall near the main exit was a white marble bust of a woman. Beneath it was a tablet, engraved.

JENNY LIND

Presented By The New York Zoölogical Society In Commemoration Of The First Appearance in America Of The Swedish Nightingale At Castle Garden.

Linny knew about Jenny Lind. She had heard about her from her mother.

The boy with the insistent fingers and the eyeglassed girl stood a moment gazing up at the bust and the placard.

"Who's she?" said the boy.

"You're asking me!" retorted the young lady, with fine irony. "It says Swedish nightingale I guess she got her dates mixed. She ought to be up in the bird house at Bronx Park."

The young man went into a flattering paroxysm of mirth. "No fun!" he said. "You're a sketch!"

I could have told him, Linny thought, hotly. I could have told him all about Jenny Lind, the way my mother told me. But then the young man would never have laughed and squeezed her arm and said she was a sketch.

When she emerged, blinking, into the mid-afternoon February sunshine, the Battery Park photographer was taking a picture. Ranged before him in a wooden pose stood the young man and the girl with the eyeglasses. They were smiling self-consciously. The photographer ducked beneath his little black cloth, he emerged with a worried look. His business instinct battled with his artist soul. The artist won.

"Lady," he demanded, mournfully, "you keeping your glasses on?"

"Sure," replied the young lady, blithely.

"Sure she's keeping them on," the young man shouted, belligerently. "Go on duck into your tent and snap it up."

The young lady smiled her reward upon her love-blinded knight.

Hold still, now!

Linny turned away in an absurd fury.

Boat for the Statue of Liberty just leaving thirty-five cent round trip! Just leaving! Statue of Liberty! Takes forty-five minutes round trip, lady. Just leaving.

The boat's cabin was hot. In every corner was a couple, low-voiced, intent. The boat's cabin seemed to be all corners all snugly occupied and each corner protected by a shimmering haze of amorous mystery.

Linny went outside, banging the door behind her, and stood, bracing herself, on the forward deck. The air was biting. The top-heavy island receded. The wind whipped her cheeks. The tears sprang to her eyes. She denied them to herself. It was the cold. This was fine.

This was what she liked. That was the Swede in her, like her mother and her mother's folks, she thought.

But when they reached the little island that held the Statue of Liberty, and the crowd swarmed up the gangplank and hurried toward the statue's base, she decided, suddenly, not to wait for the next boat, not to climb the statue's many stairs, not to see the View. She wanted to go back, unreasonably, at once, with this boat which even now was being filled with the new crowd returning from its inspection of the statue.

Two lantern-jawed military police, deceptively impressive in their olive-drab uniforms, stood guard on either side of the gangplank. From the corrugated metal shed on shore came the sound of a radio, whiling away the Sunday hours of the military police off duty. Wha-wha-wha-wha whined a crooner.

Linny turned, blindly, and stumbled down the gangplank to the boat. The S. S. *Hook Mountain* cast off.

"Take her away!" yelled the military police. Linny shrank. It was like a personal insult.

Battery Park reached, it was half-past five. The Aquarium was closed. The crowds had thinned. The air was sharp. By the time she got uptown to Werner's cafeteria it would be six. The day was nearly over.

Werner's cafeteria, uptown on Lexington, showed a half-block of cheerful plate-glass window. Those who sat within had no dietary secrets from the world.

Linny almost always ate her dinner at Werner's cafeteria. It was cheap, bright, good, clean. You got your tray, you selected your food, you served yourself. A long counter stretched the length of the farthest room. On it was ranged a bewildering variety of food. To choose amongst it was to illustrate the impressive power of decision in the human mind. Enormous roasts of beef and of pork and of lamb; pans of fish; mounds of vegetables, green, white, gold; bowls of salad; quarter sections of fruit tarts, mosaics of plum and apple and apricot; acres of coffee cake. The catch in it was that, the decision once made, the soup was found to taste strangely like the roast, and the roast like the vegetables, and the vegetables like nothing at all. Still, it was almost hot; and nourishing. The place was crowded, as always. Linny was forced to choose a table at which sat a man, eating. He kept his hat on. He ate, keeping his eyes on his food. He did not even glance up at Linny when she sat down. He was a middle-aged man. Pieces of food kept clinging to his pale tan mustache. Linny kept her eyes cast down, too.

A movie. I'm sick of movies, she said to herself. Good and sick and tired of movies. Always the same thing. All that necking. And the couples around holding hands, too, and carrying on. It was always too hot in the movies. She might go over to the room, first, and change her shoes, and rest a minute before going to the movie.

Her feet were tired, walking around all day in new Sunday pumps.

She had finished her dinner. Strawberry tart—fresh strawberries, too, in February! It had looked delectable beyond words and had tasted like raw cucumbers.

She had selected her food in silence, pointing. She had eaten in silence. She was out again in the February dusk. Suddenly, without warning, panic clutched her. You could live in New York, and go around all day, and have nothing happen. Not one thing. All day long she had talked to no one. From the moment of her awakening this morning until now, standing on the street corner in the early spring dusk, she had talked to no human being. Not one. She was a ghost, unreal, immaterial, drifting like fog through an indifferent city, mingling with the throng, but no part of it. She was nothing. She was nobody.

Chatter chatter, talk talk, laugh laugh, heh buddy where you going, what do you want to do now, let's hop a bus, meet my friend Mr. Sweeney. All about her people talked to people, walked arm in arm.

She began to run. Her face was distorted. Her head was down. She bumped into someone. It brought her to her senses. She slowed her pace to a walk, straightened her hat, her smart little spring hat that she had made herself. I guess I'm tired, standing around all day. I'll go to the room lay down on the bed a minute rest myself.

But at the thought of the room—the dark quiet little grave of a room—her footsteps lagged. Lagged. Eighty-fifth street. Eighty-sixth and Lexington.

"Hello, sister!" It was the pimply oldish man slouching there, as usual, against the pillar of the cigar store on the corner, a limp cigarette in his mouth. "Hello, sister!"

"Hello yourself!" croaked Linny, to her own monstrous surprise. Her lips were stiff with distaste.